Wolf Trails

Nik Sawe

DUNHILL

Published by
Dunhill Publishing
18340 Sonoma Highway
Sonoma, California 95476

Printed and bound in the United States of America.

Publisher's Cataloging in Publication Data

Sawe, Nik 1983 -
Wolf Trails / Nik Sawe. — 1st ed.
p. cm.
Library of Congress Catalog Number: 00-131965
ISBN 0-9701088-4-2
First Printing: February, 2001

1. Wolves—Juvenile fiction. 2. Family—Juvenile fiction. 3. Wilderness areas—Juvenile fiction. I. Title.

PS3569.A8355W64 2001 [Fic]
QBI00-500121

Cover design by Robb Pawlak

To my parents - May the trails ahead be calm and level,
and may your feet fall on the softest grass.

Chapter One

The sunlight, for a brief moment, seemed to flare upon the meadow, casting an orange glow about the pale brown grasses. Sensing that the day was retreating, the birds that had been foraging there sought safety in the leafy shelter of the black hawthorns that surrounded the clearing. Down below the sloping fields, a mouse scampered toward his hole. The tiny creature cast its eyes upwards as it was engulfed in shadow—often the sign of a hawk or owl. Yet the wolf who towered over the mouse regarded it dispassionately, quiet sadness in his gaze. The mouse paused, uncertainly twitching its whiskers as it tried to comprehend the fence which separated them. Then its curiosity gave way to fear, and it dove to the comfort of its burrow.

The wolf regarded the little tunnel for some time. Yet the mouse was not the subject of his reverie; rather, it was the safety and surety of the mouse's burrow, and the mouse's freedom to roam the meadows which lay just beyond the fence. The wolf's eyes were forlorn, and many children, if they saw such a look in the eyes of their dog, would have wept for it and nursed it until the look had disappeared. Perhaps it was because children would have cried that the wolf was kept here, locked up within the confines of a crude laboratory pen with his equally despondent family, tucked away from the sight of any child. After all, when parents fear such a beast shall arrive in the night and slay their cattle and perhaps even their young ones, it would not be right for their children to cry for the object of such fear: it would only get in the way of their own safety. And so the quiet watcher in the pen was made into something he was not: a cattle-slayer and child-stealer, one who comes out of the dark forest at night to wreak havoc. Worse yet, these lies were created by enemies whom he had never even met, men that knew little or nothing about him. The wolf in the pen, and his family, were hated unjustly by those they did not know, a hatred which raised a far greater barrier against their future than the fence which now stood in front of them.

Behind the pen was a large laboratory. The wolves did not altogether understand its purpose, only that pain often came from it, and that it was a foul place. A miasma of sickly odors emanated from it, mainly of chemicals and dogs. At any time there were about twenty dogs within, but their stock changed from week to week. The wolves in the pen could sense that the dogs within were beginning to stir, a sign that it was soon time for the humans to go home. The dogs were left unsedated during the night, since, as there were no people about for several miles, their cries of pain and frustration would go unnoticed. Of course, the wolves were greatly disturbed by the ceaseless din, but that was of no concern to the scientists, as operations were cheaper this way.

The black wolf was roused from his reverie by another who seemed in brighter spirits. "Thinking deep thoughts again, philosopher? A mouse in his burrow, now, has caught your attention? It is doubtful that he could tell you the reasons for our capture, or why the humans cut up our tails, or even why his favorite seeds are those fresh-fallen from the trees! Least of all should he tell us how to escape this prison! No, Rapid, that is a task left to one better, more quick of wit and cunning of mind. Lucky for you, my brother, I am such a one!" and with this exclamation, the wolf bowed his head low, grinning slightly as he looked up towards Rapid, the black wolf, to see what he thought of the performance.

Now, Tundra, as this other wolf was named, did not rightly *say* such things. At least, he did not in the sense that people would say something. Wolf-Speak *is* a language, but it relies upon body movements and positioning far more than actual vocalizations. Tundra had merely expressed his sentiments by the way he approached his brother, and by a few grunts. Humans have lost the ability to read all but the most basic of these body positions, which is why they rely so heavily upon words (many of those words devoid of any real substance anyway). Thus, Wolf-Speak, at best, can be translated only crudely, and though this story has embellished it somewhat, it is actually quite an eloquent language. Besides, Tundra was a master of the language, even a bit of a poet, as far as wolves go.

As Rapid regarded his brother, the last of the sunlight seemed to make Tundra's amber coat glitter. Rapid himself was by no means a pessimistic wolf, but after almost eight months confined to the little pen, he had all but given up hope. He was perhaps the most ingenious of the Copperleaf Pack, but after several months of trying to devise an escape, he had concluded that the effort was fruitless. The fence which encircled the pen held a powerful electrical current which could leave the wolves stunned for several minutes, besides being quite painful. The fence itself, fifteen feet high at least, was mounted on a thick concrete base which went below the ground farther than they could dig. Worst of all, the electrical hum of the fence constantly tormented the wolves, its high pitch never pausing to pity their sensitive ears. Only Tundra and Rapid's third littermate, Timber, refused to give up, when the rest of the pack had long ago resigned themselves to a slow fate at the hands of the scientists.

Rapid gazed into Tundra's golden eyes and tried to reason with him. "We've been about this pen a hundred times, and Timber has tried the fence twice as often. The humans' magic is far too strong to break by our deeds alone."

"Perhaps," admitted Tundra, though he still seemed sure of himself. He had begun to lead his brother towards the northeast side of the pen, and Rapid followed him listlessly. "But where we cannot break men's magic, Nature can." The tawny-colored wolf pulled to a halt in the farthest corner of the pen and looked down at the base of the fence. Though the concrete line seemed solid, the barest of two telltale cracks could be seen in the twilight.

"What do you mean?" asked Rapid, unable to grasp his brother's mysterious words. "I sense nothing here."

"Ah, but you shall. Timber will show you what I found, for I cannot get a good grip on it. Timber!" he barked, turning back towards a small rock cluster near the center of the pen which served as the pack's den. An enormous black wolf emerged from amidst the boulders. Never has the like been seen since him, nor shall it be for a great while. His muscles shone through his fur as sculpted metal would through silk. Timber was possibly the largest wolf in all of Canada, but his rugged body moved across the rocks with a quickness that belied his bulk. Rapid smiled inwardly with love for his favorite brother; they had been through many hardships together.

Tundra told Timber to demonstrate, and the big wolf splayed his huge paws across the concrete surface, looking for the right placement. Rapid grew nervous and paced in place for a moment, for Timber's paws were terribly close to the electric fence. Then, with one swift motion, Timber pulled back, taking the loose foot-wide slab of concrete with him. The stones scraped each other as they parted, and Rapid looked nervously back to the lab, hoping that the scientists hadn't heard the noise. The wolves could put their paws beneath, touching free soil.

Rapid stared in wonderment for a moment, then took up the slab himself, thoughtfully pushing it about. "Well done, poet," he said admiringly. "The pack may soon owe our freedom to you. We can easily dig a hole just large enough to get by under the fence. Keep it quiet a while, though. We don't want the humans finding this and then have everyone's spirits broken before we've even begun. It will take a day or two to work up a large enough hole to escape. Until then we must keep it a secret. We'll work on it only at night and keep it well hidden during the day, like this," and with that he and Timber nudged the concrete back into the fence's base, throwing some dirt in front of it to try and hide the disturbance.

The darkness outside, now that the sun had fallen back, was nothing compared to that which seemed to envelop the inside of the lab. It seemed as if the metal which was to be found everywhere—the instruments, the tables, the cages—simply added to the darkness and complemented the smell of Death which constantly poured from the kennels. The dogs paced about in their cages with countless ailments: one's ears were cut short to see if it affected her instinctual reflexes, three had been infected with the deadly parvovirus and then given cheap new trial treatments (to see which remedy would cost the least and still keep the dogs alive), and others were the subjects of far more horrible experiments which won't be explored here. Suffice to say that some seemed to be almost arbitrarily performed, more out of a perverse sense of curiosity than for any real scientific gain.

There were only two scientists to run the lab, for it was a small enterprise and did not wish to attract too much attention, lest publicity be accompanied by red tape. The lab was in reality a renovated barn, as its unassuming, homely exterior was all the better to hide the darkness within. The head scientist, Haxler, had begun the lab with dogs at first, which were then used in experiments to benefit drug manufacturers, and, ostensibly, humanity as well. The dogs were nearly always obtained from local animal shelters, where they were snatched from the brink of euthanasia so that, as Haxler so nobly phrased it, "they should not suffer needlessly." Of course, he did not mean that they should be free of suffering, but that there should be a need for such suffering to fulfill. Haxler was by no means a sadist; on the contrary, he was a realist. He knew perfectly well that the animals would die regardless of whether he performed his tests, and figured that he may as well make some money in the process. It was not a question of right or wrong, and he was sharply annoyed when any question of morality came into the picture, because society had raised him to be indifferent to animal suffering. He hadn't thought much about the concept, really: he just found it to be one of those ideas that some people get carried away with. Surely, animals did 'feel', at least in terms of relays from the nervous system, but what difference did that make, if they couldn't elaborate upon what they sensed?

The second scientist, Jonathan Barnes, annoyed Haxler, though there was no doubt that the doctor was very good at his job. It was just that the fellow got bouts of *sentimentalism*, of all things. Barnes figured that he needed the money (and his salary amounted to quite a handy sum), but he couldn't shake the feeling that somehow what he was doing was fundamentally wrong. Barnes worked a second job one day a week as a veterinarian in the nearest town, Dolsty. He rationalized the double lifestyle by the fact that, on occasion, he would save one animal with a medicine which, when he had tested it a month before, had killed another. Therefore he was, from a moral standpoint, no worse off.

Dolsty was a fairly small town, with only several thousand people, which relied mainly upon its ranches for income. The ranchers were not pleased with the wolf population which shared the mountains, and a wolf would be shot on sight. Periodic hunting parties also ensured that wolves didn't stay in the area for long. It didn't occur to any of the townsfolk that no one there ever actually had any livestock killed by wolves, but nevertheless it was generally agreed that wolves caused cattle deaths. Many of the ranchers were vehement wolf-haters, and so, when they had learned of the testing lab several miles away, they struck a deal with Haxler. They pooled their resources and offered him several hundred thousand dollars to rid them of the wolves, or to polarize public support so that it was unanimously against the wolves. So, he had successfully captured a pack in the mountains north of the town, brought them back, and begun a series of tests to discover the best way to conduct an anti-wolf program.

Haxler was closing up for the night, making sure that none of the dogs had died in the last few hours, when he stopped to watch the wolves in the pen outside, dimly lit by several roof halogen bulbs. They seemed to be pacing aimlessly about, but there was a look in their eyes that he hadn't seen for a long time: it whispered of determination and patience, like that of a poor laborer who has been sitting in the waiting room for several hours and won't go home until he talks with the company boss. Haxler was suspicious of this change, but dismissed it. He had never been very good at reading animals' bodies, a talent that Barnes seemed to have in greater measure. Haxler shook his head with distaste. "If they're dying on nearly every test we perform, we'll need some new specimens. We're lucky none of them died the other day when we inserted the CDL implants into their caudal glands. . . . " Haxler ran his fingers over his lower lip agitatedly, then tried to smooth down his curled black hair. He muttered to himself, absorbed in his own thoughts, "Well, we'll just have to watch and see if it makes them more submissive. The independent client wanted it to see if he could breed his wolves into his husky line easier. He doesn't want to try it on any of his own stock. It's not in line with our main program, but he's paying quite a bit for this side experiment."

Meanwhile, Jonathan was looking through his glasses at the tag number of one small little dog who was shivering uncontrollably; the dose of the experimental heart medicine was probably too high for one his size. Barnes didn't think "stock" was a fair word to describe wild animals. It implied that animals did not think or feel, but were merely investments. Animals *did* feel, which was precisely why he had chosen to become a vet. But somewhere along the way the path became muddied, and he had wandered off of it and become lost. He stuck his hand into the kennel and gave the little dog a soft scratch behind the ears, comforting it, but he knew that it would probably die by the morning. He turned his thoughts to the CDL. It seemed a harmless enough experiment, though what logic it was based on he was unsure. Not much was known about the caudal gland, which wolves have at the base of their tail. The client had taken a gamble in creating the CDL and was anxious to know if it would pay off.

Barnes was worried about tomorrow's experiment. The "aggression neurospray" was due for arrival. The ranchers had a new scheme: could a television commercial be created, decrying the evils of wolves, featuring images of a wolf slavering at the mouth, lunging at the camera? The aggression neurospray was created for just this purpose: to turn the wolf into an insane, frothing beast. But what would be left of the wolf afterward?

Haxler was completely unaware of his co-worker's despair. He grabbed his keys from one of the dissection tables, looked at some papers for the neurospray before pushing them into his weather-worn briefcase (his eyes positively danced with glee at the prospect of the next day's tests), and hastily walked out the front door. His mind was so involved in his work that he didn't even bother saying goodbye to Barnes.

As a conciliatory gesture, after he made sure that Haxler's car had gone down the drive, Jonathan threw a dog treat to each one of the haggard animals in the kennels. He knew that within a few minutes they'd all be awake, and he quickly left before the clamor could assault his ears.

"Hold on, don't be at ease yet," said Coast, a four-year-old with white fur (or what had been white before the filth of the lab had tarnished it). Coast had an air of reserved dignity about her, and was the most peaceful of the Copperleaf Pack, watching the world with calm green eyes. The wolves were waiting for the humans to depart; they all knew about the escape route now.

The bright glare of Barnes's car lights reflected red off the wolves' eyes, and several of them pawed their faces in an effort to get the blinding light out of their vision. Rapid grunted, blinking and shaking his head. "I shall be glad not to have to put up with that any longer, if we're able to get out."

"Yes, and these as well," commented Glen, the *tanah*, or male pack leader. He looked up with anger tempered by long life at the three spaced halogen bulbs atop the lab roof. "We cannot see properly with them; its too bright, and it fouls the night-vision. It is not natural."

"Do you expect this place to be natural?" exclaimed a large wolf, second only to Timber in size, who sat upon a rotting log in the far corner of the pen. His eyes glittered in the dark with bitterness at his situation. Wrath was his name, for his temper was often fierce and he was quick to anger and bear down upon others. He spent much of his time apart from the pack, watching them with leering, cynical eyes. There were few that he befriended: mainly his littermates, Rapid, Timber, and Tundra, for he was the last born; but to them he was loyal and brave in battle. He simply had little taste for being too near the others, and so life at the lab had strained his temperament harshly. He had grown bitter with all the wolves except the blithe Tundra. Wrath continued, "There is nothing natural here! The lights which blind us, the dogs and the fence which deafen us with their incessant noise! And sometimes they will even throw to us the dead corpses of the dogs to feed upon! No, that is not natural, it is not the way that we shall live. And so we shall die by it," he exclaimed with resignation. He had little hope that the good luck which found the escape route would last. At his speech, which had mainly used barks and snarls, almost all the dogs had awoken, and began to yelp loudly.

Dogs use a primitive version of Wolf-Speak, but they have borrowed much from their human masters, and have become a great deal more vocal. Because of this, many times they'll bungle up other animals' signals, though they are far better at understanding them than people are. Dogs often will communicate almost exclusively by voice, but, like people, they can speak a lot without saying much of any real value. So, they began to talk from within the lab, though these particular dogs were not all in the best mental health, and were less coherent than most.

"What? Who's there? The lights, yes, I can see them, but I can't smell them, you know—they took my nose away, put it under a box and shipped it off to the cats, you see. Cats always go for the nose, and now they've finally got it. I do hope they give it back. . . ."

"It's so very cold . . . and what're the wolves shouting at? I'd give them something to shout at, but I'm pinned down, and Rittey stole my food through the bars. Rittey's got my food, and they've got my legs. The icicles, I mean. I can't see them, but I can feel them, all along my backside. And when I try to bite them it only grows colder."

"Would you like to switch, then? I can't stand the heat. I'm wearing the sun as a hat, like my master used to do, but it's made my head fairly boiling. Perhaps the hat's too tight. . . ."

"I don't see any hat! You're daft, d'you know that? You're all out of your minds. Now, I just have to find a way to get out of mine, and I shall be free of this place. . . ."

They'd carry on like this each night, quite disturbed, and those that were new would join in within the week. Most nights the wolves would just bear it, and try not to pay attention to the horrible conversations which leaked out through the walls. Right now, however, time was of the essence, and they could not tolerate such a din. "Quiet, *teyen*!" shouted Wrath loudly. Wolves have a few unique words, often centralized to regions or even packs, and in the region around Dolsty "*teyen*" meant "domesticated" or "held by man." Soon the chatter was halted in fearful silence.

Glen thanked Wrath, then jumped atop the pen's central boulders. He was joined by the *maisa*, Paloke, his mate. The old mother wolf watched her mate, told him he could address the pack. They were the parents to all the Copperleaf wolves, and so were accorded great respect and honor by their six children. "You have no doubt heard by now the good news," began Glen. "If Nature is with us, as it seems, then we may gain freedom from this place. It has long been our wish. But if we do escape, we must not forget those who have fallen here." The other wolves lowered their heads in painful memory. Coast had lost her two littermates, and Maya, the pup, had lost her only den-sister.

Glen nodded to Timber to remove the concrete slab, and the big wolf did so. Glen was proud of his son: Timber was likely to succeed him as *tanah*. He was a far stronger animal than any other Glen had seen, and followed his intuition well in battle. Timber would be a fair ruler, and took it upon himself to acquire the input of the entire pack on every decision, as Glen did. "Coast will begin digging, then Paloke will continue as we reach harder ground. We must finish this quickly, if not tonight then by the next moonlight. Haste is a virtue; there is much to be done before the sun shines again."

The past week had been warm; warm for March, at least. The wolves hoped that this would have made the ground easier to dig through, that it would have warmed it enough so that the dirt would be penetrable. Coast and Paloke dug for some time, but soon they hit a layer of partially frozen dirt that their claws could not pull away. There was still not enough space for a wolf to fit through, and several of the pack members turned away, disappointed. Coast, her head bent, trailed her nose to the thin snow layer and kept her eyes lowered. Rapid approached her comfortingly. "It's all right, *juipah*," he whispered, using the Copperleaf word for 'quiet one'. "You did the best you could. We'll get out somehow."

Paloke was still looking down into the small hole, deep in thought. Then she took a few sniffs of the air and turned away from the fence. “Don’t lose hope, my children,” she called across the pen. “There is still a way. Smell the winds! They carry with them the scent of warm weather, yet. If we leave the stone slightly askew, perhaps the warmth can thaw the ground.”

Timber spoke up warily, “But leaving it open—the man Haxler could see, and then we would lose our chance, maybe our only chance, of escape.” Several of the wolves whined in agreement.

Glen joined his mate. “It is a risk that we must take. They will notice something amiss there sooner or later. We must escape while it is still possible. There is some truth in what you say, though, and I think there is another way of heating the ground. We could try to warm it with our paws, taking shifts, for the rest of the night. Then we can set the stone ajar only during the warmest part of tomorrow. It should keep attention there to a minimum. Rapid, I’d like you on first shift; you can awaken me when light begins to show upon the chokecherry tree.”

The wolves began to retreat beneath the boulders. Rapid called to Tundra before his brother disappeared under the rocks. “I don’t know how to thank you for this. I don’t know if I’ll ever get another chance.”

Tundra suppressed a shudder. “What do you mean?” He tried to seem light-hearted, but something dark had seized him, and hopelessness had fallen upon him. Rapid seemed to understand, and he appeared almost ready to dart away, as if he was scared of what he was about to say.

“I don’t know. Call it a premonition, I suppose,” responded

Rapid uneasily. He had gotten these feelings before, each time before darkness fell over the pack. Tundra, as their litter was very close, knew this. What would happen this time?

Tundra tried to shrug it off, laughing uneasily. "You and your premonitions! You remind me of the tale about the wolf who howled warnings against the shadows until he realized that they were his own!" He chuckled to himself, then answered Wrath's howl that he would join them in sleep soon. He darted away towards the boulders, as if fleeing a bear, and wished Rapid a hurried good-night.

Rapid placed his paws into the cold recesses of the ditch, and whispered quietly, "Yes, and then the shadows leapt out from under his feet and he understood that they were real, and so ended all that he knew."

Chapter Two

With the approach of dawn, Rapid awoke to find Coast nuzzled close to him as always. He lifted his head and she arose, sensing the movement. He glanced around the cave. Glen and Paloke were cuddled together, and the pup, Maya, a large ball of black fur now nearing a year, was curled in a corner.

Rapid smiled as he watched Maya sleep, and, as if sensing attention, her ear flicked and her eyes fluttered open. Her forepaw lazily batted the air in front of her and her eyes closed again. She let out a prolonged yawn, then focused her eyes around her. When she saw Rapid, her mouth opened good-naturedly and she pounced upon him, bowling him over. "Rapid!" she squealed.

"Hey, watch it! You're getting quite big now, pup!" he exclaimed, laughing heartily. He leaned his head back and looked farther down the little cave. "Tundra," he called, and the autumn-colored wolf opened one eye lazily, his head resting in the dirt. "You must give Maya a story. She's long awaited one, I think."

"Of course. Maya, everyone, gather about in front of the den, and I shall tell you a tale of when we were free. The tale of your birth."

Wolves have an amazing resolve to be undaunted by circumstances which may initially frighten them. Tundra and Rapid had such resolve, and in this short exchange they had mutually agreed to cast aside what had happened the night before. It could not be helped if an evil was to befall one of them. Life would continue as normal.

Wrath watched Tundra intently as his brother wove a tapestry of words and movements, reliving young Maya's birth in his memories. Wrath's demeanor softened, his hard glare slowly changing into an eager watchfulness. Tundra was perhaps the only one with whom he felt he could lower his guard. When Tundra had at last finished his story, the other wolves applauded him with licks and playful shoves.

"How are the new pups, Paloke?" Glen asked after his son had finished. Paloke's next litter was fast on their way.

The *maisa* closed her eyes and concentrated within. "They are well. There are three young ones."

Glen smiled. A good number to have; if the Copperleaf pack could escape from the laboratory, three new wolves on the hunt would be immensely useful.

Timber pushed his way through the small entrance under the boulders. "I've replaced the stone. We must wait now. Later we can remove it again so that the sun may thaw the ground beneath it."

"Let us hope that our luck does not run out before then," Wrath said grimly, pushing past the others to dwell on dark thoughts alone.

Jonathan Barnes pulled up the old dirt road to the lab. It was seven in the morning, and, he figured, far too early in the day to do what he was about to. The old, weathered building seemed remarkably peaceful at this time of day. From the road, one could not see the dirtied wolf pen and the enormous electric fence; only the meadow beyond, and the forests on either side of the Research Center, were visible. The sun had been up for some time and it cast a warm, muted glow over the lab's grey-brown slats. Barnes could almost imagine it as a place of peace and retreat. He was surprised to realize that the dogs were silent for the moment; often they would rise again after a few short hours of exhaustion once the sunlight streamed through the windows. Once he pried open the front door by its rusty handle, Jonathan finally realized where his sense of serenity was coming from: Haxler hadn't arrived to work yet.

Jonathan cast a glance out at the wolves. The auburn one was quietly walking from side to side, parading in front of the others. All of the other wolves were sitting silently, watching him as he paced. It was quite a curious show, and Jonathan paused to watch before finding the aggression neurospray. It came in a small bottle similar to those given to asthmatics, though the tube to enter the mouth was longer and smaller.

Preparing to capture one of the wolves, Barnes took down a muzzle rod and loaded the tranquilizer gun. He and Haxler could expect resistance from the animals. He was going to try and capture the white female, though she was one of his favorites. She was the calmest and therefore the easiest to spot increased aggression in.

A few moments later, Haxler walked in the door. He remarked about the weather and how today was going to be a bit warmer than even the past week, but he wasn't good for much other conversation. The only times he ever attempted to talk with Jonathan were when he was very excited about the testing, and on most of those days a wolf would die. "So, Jon, are we ready for today?" he asked cheerily.

Barnes's warm blue eyes turned hard, and the morning light reflected off them with a glint like cold steel. He had to avert his gaze from Haxler and take several deep breaths. It was bad enough that they were going to kill one of his favorite wolves only for the sake of money, but to enjoy it, to look forward not to the money but to the action! Did Haxler even understand how sadistic he seemed? It was almost a minute before Jonathan could reply with a remote "Yes."

Haxler took several steps forward, trying to peer at the downcast face of his associate with squinted eyes. His brow tightened into a suspicious frown. "Is something wrong, Jon?"

Barnes's mouth had dried out, and he quickly swallowed, then turned to face his employer with a fragile smile. "No. No, nothing's wrong." As he said those words he could feel another fragment of his heart petrify itself into stone. He loved the wolves, and he was about to betray them. Again.

"The men look like they are getting ready for something," Rapid said distrustfully. "Spread out into smaller groups, so that they don't catch us all at once."

Wrath looked at Tundra and whispered to him. "The joint pains . . . they're getting worse . . . I know it is a bad time, but . . ." The big wolf fell on his side in mute agony. Attacks of "joint pains," as he called them, happened far too often, but he could usually sneak away before the rest of the pack noticed, or feign sleep, quietly bearing the pain. He truly believed that none but Tundra knew of his weakness, but the other wolves had merely kept silent, for they did not wish to destroy his sense of dignity.

"Don't worry about it, Wrath," assured Tundra. "There, crawl beneath the rotting log over there. Timber and I will keep them away from you. Rapid! We'll form a group over here—you fellows keep near the den. Now, Wrath old friend," said Tundra, looking down as his brother fell under the log's shadow, "They'll have to go through us before they find you."

Wrath, who always acted so smug and brash, looked up to his brother in genuine thanks, touching him lovingly with his paw. Then, he shut tight his eyes, trying to draw inward, away from the men and the pain, away from himself.

Barnes's feet crunched softly in the light layer of snow which had lately been turning to slush. He was inside the pen now; the lab's side door led directly out into the wolf prison. He could see the wolves in three small groups, as if they had been playing with each other. The alpha pair were to one side, eyeing him suspiciously. Near the boulders, the juvenile, the quick black male, and the white female were all together. The white female definitely looked frightened, and as their eyes met Barnes understood the message: Free Us. It was unmistakable in its simplicity. He had to stop, unable to shoot her with the tranquilizer, while he composed himself.

Then he saw him—the wolf they had nicknamed "Giant," close to one hundred eighty pounds. The behemoth paced slowly in front of Barnes, his eyes full of resolve that said if the man advanced further he might lunge. The black wolf's lip curled in a momentary snarl, and sweat beads started to form on Barnes's brow.

Haxler approached him. The taller man's mouth spread into a grin as he stood beside Barnes, rocking back and forth on his heel, one eyebrow raised. "Well?" he asked expectantly. "Are you going to knock him out so we can get going here?"

"Its just that...well, he looks quite agitated," Barnes stuttered nervously. "I'm worried about raising the gun to him, he might even lunge. You never can be too sure with wild animals." '*Especially with all we've done to these ones*,' he added to himself.

Haxler clenched his teeth. "Honestly, sometimes I don't know why I hired you." He swore under his breath and seized the tranquilizer gun. Then, instead of shooting Timber with it, he charged at the black wolf, swinging the gun around to hit him with the butt of it. The huge wolf's head went back like a spring, and a second blow knocked him into the slush. He lay still there, and the snow about him slowly reddened. Haxler breathed heavily, and then, kneeling, grabbed the big wolf by the ear and pulled his face close to his own, to make sure Timber was unconscious. As he let the limp body drop, he turned towards Barnes. The young vet was taken back by the look of pleasure on Haxler's face—he was actually grinning! "Okay, Jon, that's done with. Now, which one did you want to get?"

⁂

Timber whined once before he collapsed, a whimper of utter confusion. Tundra was confused too, and pulled back to protect Wrath defensively, but the men moved away from the log, and the tawny wolf was left in bewilderment.

Rapid motioned that Coast and Maya should climb up the boulders, so that it might take Haxler more time to get them. He stood in front, resolving not to move, even if Haxler set upon him as fiercely as he did Timber. "Stay together, you two," he warned by the movement of his feet. "It's another of their abominable tests. They're taking Timber. If you hide behind the rocks, maybe they won't take you. Once you get behind the boulders, stay absolutely motionless."

The rest of the Copperleaf obviously knew this as well. Glen and Paloke remained frozen in the snow, Tundra stood nervously in front of Wrath, his eyes quickly darting between the two scientists.

Rapid realized as he watched them that the men were looking above him, at Coast and Maya. A tranquilizer shot was fired, and he whirled around in time to see it hit Coast. He screamed her name, but she stumbled off the boulders, hitting the ground at an unnatural angle. She whined piteously, obviously in pain. Rapid darted up the rocks, pushing Maya down and into the cave beneath, before he rushed back outside to try and protect Coast.

⁂

"She's no good now!" exclaimed Barnes, sounding frustrated but silently thankful.

"You're sure?" asked Haxler, eyeing the white wolf thoughtfully. "The limp might make her seem more dangerous . . ." Coast's hind leg was broken, but mercifully she had drifted off into unconsciousness.

"Don't be ridiculous. We need a healthy animal." Barnes looked about him, trying to find a suitable sacrifice. He found the auburn male by the log and knew that it would be him. Tundra was the calmest next to Coast, one of the few who had never exhibited any overt aggression toward his captors. "Don't worry," Barnes whispered. "Everything will be fine. You mustn't resist, little wolf. We won't hurt you." The wolf looked as if he wished to run, and watched Barnes out of the corners of his eyes, turning his head away. It almost seemed as if there was something holding him back. Barnes knew that all he had said was a lie. The aggression neurospray's effects were irreversible. Once the wolf was tested, his mind would be destroyed; whatever he had felt before would be erased forever. The wolf almost seemed to sense Barnes's thoughts, and its eyes widened in terror. Barnes motioned to Haxler, and the scientist advanced with the muzzle rod in hand.

"Watch yourself, Tundra!" cried Rapid. As soon as the humans began walking towards his brother Rapid had run to guard Coast's body, but she looked in a bad way. Rapid wondered if the humans were finally trying to kill them. "Be agile, my brother! Be strong!"

"All ri–" Tundra was cut short as the muzzle enveloped him. He struggled, bucking this way and that, rolling in the mud-splattered snow, unable to free himself. His paws flailed uselessly. "Rapid!

Wrath!" Tundra pleaded. But Wrath, only a few feet away, could not collect himself. He whined from beneath the log, trying to pull himself up against the pain. Rapid lunged for the men, but Barnes caught him with the butt of the gun. The black wolf reeled back from the blow, choking, trying to get the air back into his lungs. He watched as Wrath crawled forward on his front paws, grim determination on his face, issuing a growl-whimper in challenge to the men. But they did not heed him, and Tundra was dragged back to the lab, leaving a line of mud in the snow. Wrath was almost hysterical: the big wolf was completely helpless. Rapid barked to him, "He's not gone yet, Wrath!" And with these words he knew his premonition would come true. He stumbled helplessly forward, but Haxler simply kicked him away. He fell at the door to lab, and saw Tundra, now harnessed, being dragged onto the tiled floor. "Good-bye, dear Wrath!" he cried. And with that, the poet was gone. The door shut in Rapid's face, and he slipped into unconsciousness.

Just before he passed out, Rapid heard something odd. For the first time in his life, Wrath began to cry.

Tundra was lying in the back room of the lab. Every so often he would seize up, his muscles growing taut and his face drawing back in agony, before falling comatose. His mouth was frothing, and during times of consciousness his eyes, heavily dilated, would frantically search the room for signs of movement. The poet was dead now; all that remained was what the ranchers wanted to see. He was dying, though, before they could show the vicious creature to the world. He had performed only three minutes of the crazed, snarling rage the men felt embodied wolfkind before he had lapsed, his life-energy spent, into his current state. Beside him, in utter misery, kneeled Jonathan Barnes.

Haxler was not at all disturbed by the developments, and was talking comfortably on the phone to one of the ranchers, his feet on one of the empty kennels. It was the cage for the little dog that was shaking the night before, and who had died just an hour ago. "No, I don't think it's a bad sign at all. We'll just try again tomorrow, and give the next one a dose just before you film. I think it'll turn out quite well . . . Yes, they are quite vicious, really. Good, well, I'll call you in the morning. I'm going to work at daybreak, to see if I can figure out what went wrong with the treatment."

Barnes sighed deeply, then shut the back room door. The wolf was almost gone, though Jonathan had given him the minimum dosage. Its vital signs were low and dropping steadily. The golden eyes blinked slowly, and the wolf stared blankly into Barnes's eyes, shivering intensely. Jonathan whispered his apologies. The animal closed its eyes again, and the pulse count slowly subsided into nothingness.

Jonathan bit his lip, then threw himself down on the animal, sobbing uncontrollably. These tests were tearing him apart. This was the fourth wolf so far, and the deaths would only come faster as the program gained momentum. What would happen when this pack perished? Others would be brought in, countless wolves, seized from their dens, from the plains, from the womb. And they would all end here, by his hand.

It seemed a long time before he was able to pull himself away from the body. He blinked back the tears and returned to the main testing area. Haxler was still sitting there, almost insolently, with his feet upon the empty cage. The scientist looked Barnes over for a moment, understanding that he had wept for the dead wolf and silently despising him for it. "Another dead, eh? Damn weak pack, that one," commented Haxler unemotionally. He had seen Barnes cry for a dead wolf before, and every time he grew exceedingly more impatient with the vet. What wasted sentiment, for animals that were barely aware! "Go bury it in the meadow," he motioned. "I doubt the others will eat it, though it's a waste. I guess we *will* have to use some of the deer meat today." Barnes, defeated before he had begun, marched into the back room and dragged the dead wolf outside.

❋

Night arrived quickly for the wolves. They had seen Tundra's body dragged out into the meadow and lain in a pit. They had smelled Death upon him. There was no reason for him to die—if they had only found the loose slab a day earlier, they would have been free before he was captured.

Wrath lay hunched by Rapid's side, his tail low and his demeanor humbled. He felt shamed by his actions, that he had not saved his closest friend and brother. Now he believed he had to meet the next test, escape, with some sort of valorous deed. The wolves were arranged in a cluster near the concrete slab. The warmth of the day had indeed done its job, and though digging would take time, at least it was now possible. Barnes had put Coast's leg in a cast (the wolves assumed it was another test and not an act of mercy), so Paloke was left to do the digging.

The *maisa* panted heavily. The hole was quite deep now; it had to be, for the wolves did not want to be electrocuted by the fence on their way out. The first beginnings of light streamed in from below the tree line, and Glen looked toward them with fear. "It is almost finished," Paloke barked. The dogs answered this comment with a stream of questions, but the wolves ignored them.

The rest of the pack waited tensely as the morning light became ever brighter. Finally, Paloke ducked beneath to freedom with an exultant cry.

"Just in time," growled Wrath. "Quick, let us go."

Glen began to choose the pack's order. "Let Maya out, and then Rapid to guard her. Coast, too, as she is wounded." The *tanah* paused for a moment, pointing his ears past the lab. "The men are coming!"

Rapid was shocked. "So early! But how? And why could we not hear them before?"

Glen shouted, "Don't question the ways of men. Follow your mother into the eastern forest. Be swift, and do not wait for us!" The *tanah* looked at his other sons as the car pulled in the dirt road. "*Honovi*, *Hluri*," said Glen lovingly, using their pack names. "You two are the strongest. Can you make out alone? I must help Paloke with the unborn pups."

Timber and Wrath looked at each other. They were both eager to recover from their failure the day before. The car had stopped in front of the lab now. "We shall not fail you, father," said Timber in parting. As they lost sight of Glen amongst the trees the two turned to see Haxler, cursing and running into the lab. Timber sucked in his breath. "It will not be long before he is able to put us to sleep. Get through while you still can."

Wrath ducked under the fence, but in his haste he rose too quickly, and the fence stunned him. His body fell limp, blocking the hole.

Timber growled in frustration, looking back at the lab. One of the dogs warned him, "He won't put you to sleep, you wolves. He's got the loud stick, the one that kills." Haxler had worried about this moment. If the wolves escaped, CDL implants still unchecked, the townsfolk might learn the nature of the experiments and shut the lab down out of sheer panic. It would be better to kill the wolves and be done with them.

The first shot fired, and Timber's feet buckled under him at the sheer noise of the blast. He reeled upwards as if he had been shot, completely deafened. He thought of the pain Haxler had caused the Copperleaf, the brothers and sisters lost, the constant pain in his tail, the savage beating the day before. In the painful silence he decided what he must do.

The gun fired again, the shot again landing wide of Timber, spewing up mud into the air. Then the huge wolf charged, throwing his bulk through the window and onto Haxler, sprawling the man backwards across test tables and into the opposite wall. Kennels collapsed about them, and the dogs shouted more than ever before, though Timber could not hear them. He gazed at the man's limp body, surprised now at how little fear it inspired, and slowly stumbled out the back door.

Wrath met him, crawling out from beneath the fence. In due time Timber was able to hear his brother speak. "What of Haxler?"

he asked in fear.

"I . . . don't really know. I think he is dead now. I don't want to go back in there."

The wolves stood there, near the meadow, looking into the sky, while they recovered from their ordeal. The birds, the voles, the far-off scent of mule deer—it all seemed tangible now, where before the sights and scents were nothing more than whispers of a dreamworld. "I smell blood on you, brother," mentioned Timber worriedly. Wrath turned around, showing him his tail, where blood trickled through his fine guard hairs onto the spotless white flowers below. The first shot, at least, had struck its mark.

They ran up the meadow, truly happy, their tongues lolling out. It seemed as if they were lighter now, that life had returned to them. The other wolves were waiting for them at the edge of the forest, and all started to head southeast through the underbrush. One, however, hung back from the rest. Rapid recalled the words he had spoken to Tundra: "The pack owes our freedom to you." He thought of those words, thought of the terrible price freedom had cost. Silently, standing upon the flowered slope, he paid his respects to his dead brother.

Chapter Three

The pack was free now, and the wolves absorbed the beauty and diversity of the wilderness with a sense of unreality. For eight months they had only beheld the small meadow, and then only from behind a fence. They had long since forgotten the wonderful feel of undergrowth beneath their feet. The sight of a snowshoe hare which watched them tensely before it darted down a woodland path awakened long-dormant impulses, and the uninjured pack members pursued it for some time, exercising their legs with the easy hunt.

The wolves had headed due east from the meadow for several miles before pausing to rest, for many of the pack still felt their wounds. Timber was bruised and sore from facing Haxler the last two days, and Coast loped along on three legs, holding her right forepaw tentatively in front of her. Wrath's wound was of no consequence to the trek, though he was quieter than usual, as it is difficult for a wolf to communicate without the use of his tail. Paloke was heavy with the pups and tired easily, unused to such walks, for the Copperleaf pack was generally out of shape from the time spent in the lab. They would often nudge the scars in their tails, for they could tell that something unsettling was concealed beneath. The wolves had stopped amongst some tall fruit-bearing trees, and they looked about them in quiet admiration of Nature. The sunlight trickled down between the leaves, lighting them in gold-green splendor, and as the wolves regarded each other they saw that each seemed to swim in the light: the swaying branches constantly changed the shadows, almost as if they were beneath a sea of trees.

Glen and Timber consulted each other on the best path to take. They had decided to return home. Haxler was most certainly dead, Glen assured his son, and it didn't occur to the wolves that the scientists would first seek them where they had originally caught them, not far from the old den. Therefore they decided to return to their home, and late in the afternoon started to head southeast.

By the late evening, when the crickets' chirp filled the woods, the wolves had found their way back to the old den. It was no more than a large hole in the ground in the corner of a small clearing. Paloke immediately descended to check if it was still intact, and though several rats had to be driven out and the roof had caved in halfway through the main passage, the den seemed as before. Paloke quickly pushed the fallen dirt to one side, following the corridor upwards, before curling up comfortably in the back and falling asleep.

Maya, although she had hardly been two months old at the time of their capture, was greatly comforted by the prospect of home. She climbed to the crest of a hill and pranced atop it lightly, nipping at butterflies, her black fur shining silver in the afternoon light. The other wolves followed suit, and soon most were racing about the woodland, playing fiercely in mock battle with each other. The elk watched warily as the pack broke into a large field where they were roaming, but the wolves paid them no heed. Wild animals are far more involved in the Now than people are, for the exact hour is of no consequence. The belly will tell them when they are hungry; the mind, when they are tired.

At last, exhausted, the wolves returned to the densite, collapsing noisily into the fallen leaves. Glen, however, raised his nose suspiciously, and then bade his children to stay behind. Of all the wolves, he had retained his instincts the most, and now he had sensed a faint presence amongst the winds. He ran south through the pines, his eyes shifting constantly, trying to seek the source of the troubling scent amidst the undergrowth. The shadows seemed suddenly like great beasts drawn onto the forest floor who leapt out at him angrily, trying to seize his paws. Glen could tell by the rising of the fur on his back that the presence was near. The animal—whatever it was—was skilled; it did not show itself, and was careful to remain downwind of Glen, so as not to stir him with its smell. The wolf stopped, making no sound, listening carefully. His powerful muzzle opened in a false yawn to display his enormous teeth. But the pursuit continued. Whatever was stalking him was an expert, and its paws were placed on only the softest soil. Then, the winds shifted, and Glen caught scent of the animal. The old *tanah* growled frustratedly, "*Teyen girim yopah mirikwed.*"*

As noiselessly as it had approached him, the big dog leapt, knocking Glen sideways. The wolf snarled, rolling away from his assailant. He lashed blindly upwards into air, forcing his paws out

---

* "There is a dog amongst the shadows."

to try and strike the dog. But the animal was already behind him, its teeth gripping his shoulder and pulling roughly back, trying to drag him away from his position and down into a muddy ditch to the left. Both canines fell below, Glen landing dazed upon the soil, grit in his eyes and mouth. The dog stood over him, roughly tossing him onto his back. Its paw pushed onto his throat, its crushing weight dizzying the wolf. Glen's head reeled onto the ground, and he closed his eyes. "Defeated by a mere dog!" he thought to himself. "Perhaps my time is passed. It is not a fitting ending for an old warrior like me, but if I deserve it the pack is better off without me." He waited for the killing blow, but it was delayed, and he attempted to kick the dog with his hind legs and wriggle out of the hold, but the *teyen* would have none of it. It just stood there, pushing harder and watching him silently.

Glen looked up at the dog. He was for the most part white, but spotted with the color of fall leaves, and one ear fell rakishly over his face. His eyes danced with quiet amusement as Tundra's had, and it almost seemed to Glen as if the dog was laughing at him. So would the rest of the pack if they got word of this embarrassment. "Look here, this has gone on enough, *teyen*," said Glen angrily. "Either let me up and I shall leave you alone, or kill me. Be quick in your decision, lest it be your downfall." Glen tried to snap at the dog's forelegs and draw out from under it, but the dog darted back and jumped in again before the *tanah* could get away, this time gripping the back of Glen's neck with his teeth. Try as he might, Glen could not shake the dog, and as the dog's teeth tightened, Glen sank down into the ditch again. The dog pressed forward, pushing the wolf's face into the mud.

"Now, *you* look here, wolf. I think I'm in charge," the strange dog asserted. "You've made several mistakes already. The first was trying to track me when I was downwind, and this far away from your den, too. The second, and by far the worse, was calling me *teyen*. I'm not a *teyen*, mind you. The last wolf that tried to say so lost his throat before he could finish. Men rely on me, *not* the other way around, and I give them help only when I wish it."

Glen was puzzled by the dog's speech. This animal was certainly not like the dogs at the lab; no, this dog was actually coherent in his statements. And he sounded like a forest hunter, not some silly yap from a back porch. Still, the *tanah*'s spirit could not be broken, though he was suffocating with his face plunged into the mud. "That is what all *teyen* say—" began the wolf, before the dog's teeth dug farther into the back of his neck. He could feel the blood running down the sides of his throat, mixing with the muddy pools beneath.

"Stop there, wolf. I wouldn't wish to kill an old-timer like you. I'm sure you've seen some fine battles. Still, I sense you're not one to talk. You have the smell of a *teyen* about you yourself. Now, what's the story behind that, I wonder?" The dog dragged Glen out of the mud, and the wolf gasped for breath. The mutt was still standing on him, staring at him eye-to-eye, but the wolf made no attempt to speak.

Just then the leaves above the ditch crunched heavily. Both canines leapt to their feet. It was Wrath, staring smugly down at the two. "Glen? Is that you?" he sniffed, almost mockingly. "Looks like you're in a position now, eh? How entertaining it would be for *me* to be the *tanah*!"

The dog chuckled as Wrath jumped easily down into the ditch.

"You're a pack leader, name-caller?" he asked with surprise. He pushed Glen out from under him, and the wolf immediately jumped to his feet beside Wrath. Yet the mutt did not seem ill-at-ease, even against two wolves—giants of their kind, no less. "I'm sorry to have caused you so much trouble, Glen-*tanah*. But it turns out that you're just the one I'm looking for, after all."

Wrath, now that he had finished laughing at his father's vulnerability, turned suspiciously upon the stranger. "And why would you be looking for him? You're awfully cheeky for a *tey*-" Glen silenced his son before he could continue.

The dog's eyes narrowed with hostility toward the newcomer. "You smell more of one than I. But we went over that already, before you got here. Why am I looking for him? Certainly not to kill him; I would've done that already. I'm interested in joining your pack, or at least I was until you opened your mouths. I scented you earlier this morning, and I've been tracking you for the better part of the day. Seems like you're new in the area, and might need some help in the local territory, though you found that abandoned den fast enough."

Wrath was staring incredulously at the dog. "You want to join our pack? But you're a . . . a dog! You'll go crazy inside a week, and start spouting gibberish. Besides, what use could we have for *your* skills? We're old paws at this place. Bred and born here. We only haven't been around lately because. . . ."

Glen silenced his son again. "We have been, er, journeying. We lived at the 'abandoned' den about the same time a year ago. Though I doubt you're more than a yearling yourself, and new at the forest, at that," he said disdainfully. All wolves display a certain condescension when dealing with dogs, for they believe that dogs are merely the stupid, fawning servants of man. Glen had already forgotten that this dog had laid him flat on his back but spared his life not a moment before.

"Hardly," answered the dog. "I've seen a fair number of seasons, myself. But your smell isn't quite the same as the one at the den. Though now that you mention it, I can see the resemblance. You're almost like faint shadows of it, however. I don't rightly know how to explain it."

"You needn't worry about such things," said Glen hastily. "They don't concern you. But joining the pack, why, that's absurd! For your sake, I must say you cannot, benevolent though your intentions may be."

The dog paused and snorted impatiently, then turned around in place. "I thought I had already proved my worth to you. Sneaking up on a *tanah* is not often an easy task. But it is no matter. I'll tell you what: let me live with you for several days, and if some of the pack still wishes me ill will, take me on a hunt. I shall show you what I'm really capable of."

Glen had the last word in such matters as these, and Wrath could do nothing but give the dog a bitter look. Glen hesitated, looking the dog over. He was handsome in appearance, almost comical with his one floppy ear, but a strong dog nonetheless, a mix of Husky and some other, burlier mountain breed. And he had already shown his skill in stealth and battle. The old wolf broke into a grin, his tail slowly swaying. He cocked his head to one side and his wizened eyes, set deep behind the whitening muzzle, met the young dog's. "We cannot call you *teyen*, as you have stated clearly.

What, then, do you wish to be called?"

The dog cocked his head to one side and panted happily, bounding out of the ditch and turning as if to run. At the last minute he cast his head back to the two grey figures standing in the mud pit. "*Teyen* I am not, yet I shall go by the name my master has given. I am known as Salyr."

Wrath whined, deep in the thrall of his joint pains. Salyr remained near his side, watching his every move, as Tundra used to. The two had grown remarkably close in the past week, and Wrath had opened up to the dog with a bond alike to that which he had only shared with Tundra. Salyr's wry humor had reminded the entire pack of their lost brother, though the emotions that this similarity evoked were mixed. The dog soon heard the history of the pack's harrowing escape from the lab, and was a good deal more respectful of them afterward.

"Are you sure you're all right? Perhaps if we threw you into the Washbourne it would do you a bit of good. You know, like bath salts," jibed Salyr.

"No, I don't know. You're quite odd, with all your Man-Speak, dog," Wrath said irritatedly. "Sometimes I think you're rather mad."

Maya, who was nearby, trotted over. "No, he's not mad. He's much different from the dogs at the lab." The little black yearling turned curiously to Salyr, searching his countenance thoughtfully. "You don't bark, do you, unless there's a point? The fellows at the lab were odd that way, you know, for they'd often bark at the wind or the ground."

Salyr laughed. "No, I've not fallen that wrong in the head. The Copperleaf must have had a rough time in that lab, though. How did you stay sane?"

Wrath lay on his side, gazing blankly ahead in memory. "It was difficult. One of us, early on, did go quite mad. She couldn't handle it, I suppose. The men—they had changed her somehow." The big wolf grew silent, caught up in pains past and present. "They changed all of us," he whispered. "And now the forest feels different. I wonder if we even belong here any more."

Salyr was disconcerted by his friend's talk. "Sleep for a while," he comforted him. "It will do you some good, and you'll feel better when you wake." The dog got up and left his friend to rest, motioning Maya to follow.

Wrath couldn't shut his eyes. "Damn them all . . . sleep won't solve it. The feeling won't go away—the men won't go away."

Glen trotted up to the dog as he was leaving Wrath. "You may have to prove yourself soon. Just a warning, for I think many of the pack are skeptical about you."

"Don't worry on my account," answered Salyr confidently. "I've brought down the big game before, and alone at that."

The *tanah* didn't doubt it. "Right now, though, I was curious about how close you are to men. Do you go into town often?"

"Why? What do you wish me to do?"

"Scout around for food. Men sometimes kill deer, I've heard, crushing them with large, bright beasts and leaving them upon their stone paths. I was wondering if you could find some for us."

"I suppose so, though roads aren't the safest places to go after food. I haven't seen my home for about a month now, but they usually give me a meal when I visit. They know I'm a loner." The dog's coat, rough and sticky with dirt, confirmed that he had been afield far too long. He darted away from the den, not to return for several days. Many of the wolves figured he had slipped back to humankind, that he had been nothing but a fraud, pretending that he knew the ways of the forest. More clever than most dogs, but certainly no better, the pack concluded.

The dog ran up the embankment late one afternoon, dragging behind him a large hare. "I brought this for Paloke," he announced as he arrived at the den. "I figured she needs some strength for the pups."

"What of the deer, Salyr? Did you find any?" asked Glen.

Timber, who strongly disliked dogs in general and most of all the swaggering newcomer, chimed in gruffly, "He probably ate it all, or gave it to his *master*. And why do we need *human* food? We can go hunting easily enough without taking handouts from people!"

Glen had simply wished to test the dog's loyalty, to see if Salyr would still wish to stay with the Copperleaf even when given an excuse to return to his home. Yet he did not want to embarrass the dog by saying this.

"Timber, calm down," said Salyr uneasily. His voice seemed anxious to make peace, but his body was poised for a counterattack. He was not willing to show weakness to one who mocked him, even if he was the largest wolf in Canada. "I found a deer, all right, but it is far south of here. And roads are dangerous places to eat, anyway. My advice would be each to grab a little meat, dart away, and cache it somewhere. It's really not worth the danger, and I do agree with Timber: hunting is far easier than trying to maneuver around human roads."

"Then perhaps you'd like to show us how to hunt?" asked Timber. "You must be quite good at it, to live in the wild for a month at a time. There's a field of voles not far from here where you could show us your amazing tracking skills."

Wrath approached his brother, his gold eyes menacing. He shook his head upwards. "Don't do this, *Honovi*. He is my friend, and you know you do not wish my anger upon you." This seemed only to make Timber more hostile, for he felt this meant that the dog was replacing Tundra in Wrath's eyes.

Salyr growled threateningly at Timber's taunt. "Wolves of your kind often seem very prejudiced against—"

"Creatures who ally themselves with men?" said Timber, a low rumble, as that of approaching thunder, building in his throat. He moved closer, with deliberate steps toward the dog. Salyr, though he was of enormous size himself, was dwarfed by the titan wolf, but his feet remained firmly planted in the ground and his tail remained high. Timber's teeth were bared and his tongue darted out from between them, his growl escalating. "Yes, as well we should be. Many of our kin have been slaughtered by them. Remember Tundra?" he turned cruelly to Wrath, seeing that his point had struck its mark. The big wolf lunged at Timber, but Timber's sheer strength overcame him, bearing down upon his brother in a snarling rage. Wrath usually had his temper to his advantage, but Timber, seeing Salyr only as the epitome of the horrors that men had brought upon the pack, was equally frenzied. Wrath nonetheless slashed a deep wound across his brother's chest, one that would doubtless leave a scar. In a matter of moments, however, Wrath was bent down in the grass, his ears grudgingly turned back, looking up at Timber for mercy. The enormous black wolf whispered into his brother's ear as he watched Salyr hatefully, "This human-plague must be purged. It has affected our minds and our judgment. Nowhere is this more apparent than in the dog. He is a traitor to all that came from wolves, and has struck a bargain with the very animals that killed our brother and sisters. You are friends with a *teyen*! You used to despise them. Tundra's death has wounded you much, and that is natural: It is part of the healing process. But do not betray his ideals and throw out his memories to consort with this man-made jester! I fear that the weakness that has befallen you and Glen to drive you to this madness will only spread, and it shall be our downfall."

Wrath's eyes were smoldering with indignation, but before he could devise a rejoinder the big wolf had left him lying in the grass and was walking steadily towards Salyr. The dog pulled back, every muscle a taut string, prepared to lunge at his opponent. The other wolves watched, and knew that if Timber decided to attack the dog, the battle was already decided. Rapid quickly moved next to his father.

"He will kill the dog, if you don't stop him," said the sleek black-haired wolf resolutely.

The old *tanah* sat motionless, watching as his son advanced upon Salyr with mounting hatred. "Salyr wished to join us, and must take whatever Nature places in his way," he answered.

Rapid understood that Glen would do nothing. "Timber! Stop this madness! Challenge him to a hunt!"

Timber, not turning aside, quickly said, "I shall challenge him to more than that." Without breaking stride, he met Salyr as the dog tried to rush at him, grabbed the dog by the chest, and tore upwards, sending Salyr flying into a bush, a gaping wound along his breast. The young dog gasped for air, struggling helplessly to get out of the bush. Timber continued to rush towards him, this time grabbing him by the nape of his neck and tossing him into the ground, tearing into his fur. The other wolves noted that the dog made no sound in pain.

Finally, Salyr was able to roll to the side, and he jumped high into the air, landing on top of Timber. Gasping and coughing, he managed to grip the wolf's back, his teeth digging through muscle. Timber howled in pain. "Now, stop, Timber, and take care to watch your back, lest I break it."

Wrath cheered his friend, and Salyr fell, half-dead, from Timber. The wolf looked grimly at his assailant, then motioned approvingly. He was a warrior, and as such could see the worth in his opponent. Salyr had earned his respect, if not his trust. Without a word, the other wolves began to disperse from the scene. Yet Salyr called out to Timber before the wolf left. "We shall hunt upon the morrow, so I may prove to you that I may help the pack, instead of simply tear it apart." The black wolf nodded soundlessly, his eyes dispassionate. Coast arrived to tend to his wounds, for both Salyr and Wrath had done him considerable damage. Wrath trotted up to Salyr, breathing heavily in the blood-soaked earth, and began to lick his friend's injuries. The dog had been able to fight Timber, and defeat him, where even bears had not. Despite his injuries, he would hunt the next day. How little his worth needed to be proven!

Chapter Four

Wrath and Salyr had stayed close together that night, elaborating on past glories. They had slept deep in the fields, but the pack paid no heed: Wrath was always the one to stay away from the den, and Salyr was as yet still an outsider.

As usual, Maya was the first one up. The boisterous energy of youth showed no indication of slowing in her: a good sign for the welfare of the pack, despite the fact that she was slight of build. "Today is the big hunt!" she yelped excitedly, stumbling over Rapid on her way out of the den.

"Yes, only must you announce it so loudly?" asked Coast, startled out of her sleep by the sudden activity.

Timber grumbled and shook himself outside the den, making way so that Maya could exit. "The dog will discover he's not a wolf, finally," commented Timber, stretching painfully.

"Hmm," remarked Glen thoughtfully, opening one eye. He rolled onto his back and squirmed about in some foul-smelling shrubbery in order to mix his scent. "He's proven he's not afraid of death, and he can handle himself in a fight. I just hope he's not in over his head. Today we go after the big game."

"At last, some real meat for a change!" exclaimed Rapid happily.

"Haven't had any deer since the old man-kill from the lab. I've eaten enough rodents to last me till the leaves fall!"

"Salyr and Wrath are still out in the field," mentioned Coast. She began to howl, and the whole pack joined in suit. A brief howl answered them, and in a moment the two canines trotted up to the densite.

"All right, we should probably search out into the northeast, at the feet of the hills. We often found game there in days of old," said Glen.

Salyr seemed ill-at-ease, but Timber stared grimly at him, warning him that the wolf did not wish to hear what he had to say.

Glen brightened, walking up to Maya and playfully nuzzling her. "It will be Maya's first real hunt." Maya pawed her father's muzzle joyfully, then danced around in circles, tail wagging excitedly. The first hunt was a major turning point in a wolf's life, and the others, even Salyr, congratulated her on the occasion.

All the wolves—sans Paloke, as they did not wish to risk the unborn pups heavy within her; and Coast, with her wounded leg—departed with tremendous speed. They smelled the air and the tracks on the ground as they ran in loose formation, and none needed to request direction; they could already smell their quarry more than four miles away: a moose, rank with sickness, and its calf.

In less than an hour the wolves reached the small pond where the moose and calf grazed upon some water plants. Glen peered from across the pond at the two animals, who had not noticed the pack yet. "This looks like a good prospect, though it is quite far from the den. I doubt we can bring meat back to the others. Maya, I don't want you to attack the mother; we must stall her so that you and one of the others—Rapid, I suppose, will want to—can aid you in bringing the calf down. Then we must fall back until the mother leaves, which may be some time. Timber, Wrath, Salyr, come with me. We shall charge."

With a gruff bark meant to alert the moose, the four canines leapt out to catch the attention of the mother, standing shoulder-deep in the stagnant green pond. The moose let out a snort of surprise, then advanced, feinting a charge, to protect its baby. Rapid and Maya proceeded to flank the pond, careful to keep out of smelling range of the mother. The calf was standing uncertainly at the edge of the bank, unsure of what it should do. Rapid instructed Maya as they went, completely silently, in the body-hunting language of the wolf. They moved almost as one, responding to the rest of the pack as they faced off against the mother moose with an uncanny instinct, though they could not see each others' positions.

The cow moose decided to charge, hurtling out of the pond towards the wolves and letting fly with its front hooves. Timber was struck a glancing blow where Wrath had slashed him the day before and growled in pain, remaining on the ground. The others scattered, only to come back and slash at the moose's flanks. Confused, assailed from many sides at once, it looked from one attacker to the next. None of the wolves did any real damage; they simply meant to draw its attention away from the others, so that a directed attack could not be made against any one of them. Salyr, however, jumped onto the cow moose's back, tearing deep into her hide. The moose bleated, then reared up, but Salyr held on. The other wolves were stunned at the ferocity Salyr had shown. The moose, seeing Glen to its left, finally found a definite animal on which to take out its aggression. It charged toward him, and he tucked his tail beneath his legs and bolted into the trees on the bank, not stopping to look behind him.

Rapid checked the other wolves' progress, noticing that their defense line had now broken. The cow moose would soon turn back and retreat with her young. He and Maya had to hasten. "Now, watch me, pup. Stay low, let the reeds cover you as you advance. Nature has created them just for you, to hide you so that you may catch food and live. Everything around you Nature has placed to sustain you. Watch the calf carefully . . . It has spotted us now! Dash forward, Maya! We must bring it down before the mother is able to aid it."

Maya leapt forward, jumping on top of the calf. The calf was still quite bigger than Maya herself, and thrust out with its hoof, striking Maya on the back leg. She yelped and fell into the sand. Rapid rushed forward to make sure the youngster was all right. "The hunt, it is all that I imagined, Rapid!" she exclaimed. "Quick, before it's lost!" And she continued the pursuit as the calf stumbled away, bleating frantically.

The mother moose heard its young's cries. Wrath, who had been occupying it by dodging its front hooves, knew what would happen next. He leapt to the side, the pond's green algal froth blinding his eyes as he fell beneath it. The moose would have trampled him, and it rushed straight toward its calf. But the calf was already lost, for Maya had darted beside it in a long, loping run, and as she flanked the calf her jaws found its neck and it sank underneath her steady grip.

Salyr had, amazingly, remained stuck to the back of the sickened mother moose, even during its charge. Now, as Maya and Rapid darted away from it, it let out a long, sad call, stopping before its calf. Then the moose, consumed with rage, sought to kill the dog that remained stuck to its back. With sudden insight it rushed into the pond and lowered itself beneath. Salyr, sputtering, released his hold and rose up to the surface. His feet could not quite touch the bottom of the pond, for the two animals had landed in the deepest portion, and so he helplessly tried to swim away, the stagnant water biting into his wounds, as the huge moose rose behind him. It tried to crush beneath its powerful hooves, but the dog dove beneath the water until he reached ground where he could stand, and turned to meet the cow moose. It halted, puzzled at his action, wondering why he did not run. As it raised its hoof to deliver the final blow, he leapt out of the water, grabbing onto its throat until the cow moose, too, sank slowly down. All that was left was a hulking mass, resting limply above the pond waters.

The dog crawled out of the pond, panting with exhilaration, his one floppy ear covering an eye. He looked from one to the other of the wolves as they regrouped, but none, not even Wrath, regarded him favorably. He remained at the side of the bank, his coat sopping green, utterly confused.

Glen watched the dog carefully until it was clear to him that Salyr did not understand what he had done wrong. "You have created Waste, Salyr. The cow moose could have been outrun, for you had reached level ground. Waste is a man-thing, and it is evil. That moose would have borne more young next year, or been a good meal in the fell of winter. Now, we have no need for it, and it will rot in that pool. You must learn not to bring the Waste upon our prey, or you will have no place amongst my pack."

Timber smiled smugly as the tired pack turned to their meal. He had been proven at least partially right, and the others would not forget it. As for Salyr, he had been humbled by Glen's reprimand.

The wolves ate quickly, for they knew that the smell of blood would draw other competition to the site, perhaps even grizzly bears. Then the Copperleaf quickly cached what meat they could in the woods and started back to the den.

The pack was uneasy as they returned from the hunt. During their pursuit of the moose, traveling quickly as they were, they hadn't paid much attention to the marks around the tree line which told of another pack. Surely the Copperleaf had noticed them, but they had figured, not actually smelling any other wolves, that they were safe to trespass quickly on the other pack's land. Yet, now they sensed that other animals were closer by; perhaps they had caught the intruders amongst the winds.

Glen halted to sniff at a marking along the side of a boulder. "This isn't good. That pack seems to have an enormous range, and it infringes upon our old territory considerably. They've taken the whole north and east areas of our region."

Salyr approached the boulder. "I was going to warn you earlier. The Frostwind, you know. I've tangled with them quite a few times."

The other wolves seemed more at ease. "The Frostwind, eh?" asked Timber. "We've defeated them many times. They're few in number, though they're skilled in battle. They won't attack the six of us."

"Don't be so sure," admonished Salyr. "They've increased their ranks considerably since last year. Three of their young ones have become strong, dangerous fellows. They caught some loners wandering about the edges of their range and adopted them into the pack, every one that they could get. One of them was even pregnant, and they've got two litters on the way this season." Some of the pack snorted with disbelief, as it is frowned upon in wolf life for any female but the *maisa* to bear young. "Yes, I know," said Salyr sympathetically. "Not very wolf-like behavior, certainly. But I remember they were quite bitter about always being thrust northward by you. They're bent on having a fighting pack; these days the Frostwind are all about expansion. They have at least ten wolves ready for battle, and there'll be two more right after birthing time. I'm surprised they haven't sent you packing out of your old den yet."

"Their northern boundary is within half a mile of our den," noted Glen. "They haven't left us much room. We don't want to be too far north, as we'd be nearer to the lab. Rather them captured than us, if that's started again."

"I wouldn't wish it upon any wolf, father," whispered Rapid quietly. "Haxler is dead, but other men can easily take his place."

Glen hesitated before he continued. "Nonetheless, we need to pass through their territory to get home. If we try to go around these marks, I don't know how long it will take to get back to the den. Salyr?"

The dog sat on his haunches thoughtfully. "It may be as many as ten miles if we try to navigate about the southern tip, and we're halfway home already. They are nearby, though."

Timber was sniffing suspiciously. "Greymane still rules them, doesn't he?"

Salyr nodded shortly. Timber snorted in frustration. "I suppose we should take the chance. We won't be able to travel far, being so full. Conversely, it'll be difficult to fight well after a meal, and we're wounded. Glen must make this decision."

Glen paused. "Every moment we waste here, they are coming closer. With Greymane in charge, they'll pursue us out of their range. We've trespassed once and that's enough to get his hackles up. We must travel fast, and hope that we get clear of them and into our own territory in time."

The pack trotted past the markings, each paw stepping over the imaginary wall as if it was a rope drawn taut across their path. Then, with a haste which weighed painfully upon their full stomachs, the wolves darted through the underbrush, ever listening and sniffing the air for signs of the Frostwind. After a time the wind changed and it became impossible to locate the other pack. The Copperleaf closed formation, sticking nearer to each other.

The pack was no more than a quarter mile into Frostwind territory when they found themselves approaching a pass, a deep trench in the earth on the sides of which stood two enormous hills. They were in open ground, and the pack found this not to their liking. The Frostwind scent was growing ever stronger, and the Copperleaf were ill at ease, for it seemed as if the other wolves were all around them.

Suddenly a rallying howl erupted from either side of the trench, and it seemed as if the hills had become a mass of wolves. Both black and grey animals quickly surrounded them, and the Copperleaf formed a defensive ring. Glen glared determinedly at an enormous wolf, salt-and-pepper colored, who stood atop the hill. It was Greymane, who was not senior to Glen in years but who certainly was superior in tactics.

"Glen!" the wolf exclaimed. Greymane's voice had a sing-song lilt to it which gave him an air of insincerity. His followers were circling the Copperleaf's ring now, seeking an opening. Maya realized with horror that they had become the hunted. "It has been long," Greymane continued. "Though your departure was not mourned, you understand. You may find, old wolf, that many things have changed since you left. For instance, if someone has gall enough to enter my realm without my leave, I will kill him without a thought. You can no longer send my pack scattering to cower among the bushes. It appears you have lost some of your number, although I have only prospered from your absence." The Frostwind closed in, feinting inwards towards the ring, trying to draw out the Copperleaf to gain an opening. The Copperleaf held fast. "Yes, many things have changed," muttered Greymane to himself, sounding almost like a bird. "Remarkable! You, Glen, smell of *teyen*! The odor is unmistakable!" The peppered *tanah*'s head darted back with surprise. "And you even have a *teyen* with you! Hullo, Salyr! Haven't learned to stop searching for scraps along my borderlands, eh? Well, we'll soon see to that, won't we? Fill the gully with their blood!"

As the pack was beset on all sides—Rapid counted nine wolves, but there may have been more that he couldn't see—Maya whispered to Timber, "Quite bent on speeches, isn't he? He seems more of a *teyen* than we! Full of silly sayings with very little substance."

Timber's eyes did not waver from the approaching wolves, and he lunged out, wounded as he was, to seize one by the leg and cripple it, sending it howling away. He slashed a second across the chest, knocking it back against the ravine bank, before he deigned to answer. "Perhaps, though his strategies are almost as complex as those of men. Yet his overconfidence does him disservice, as it does with men." As he said this, the huge wolf lunged out to grab an adversary by the tail, pulling it away from Wrath. The two collapsed in a writhing mass of black fur.

"Glen! Break formation!" cried out Salyr, as two snarling grey wolves began to drag him toward the Frostwind's main line. The defensive ring was breached, and the Copperleaf scattered, battling alone and in twos as the enemy closed in. Greymane watched smugly from above. Then, his tail swishing lightly behind him, he called two burly fellows to him, and the three descended the hill together to finish off the Copperleaf.

Yet Glen's pack was far from defeated. They had slain one of the eleven wolves at the first advance, and even now two more had retreated from the fight, too wounded to continue. Wrath and Rapid had rushed to Salyr's aid, tearing the other wolves off him. The dog was exceedingly weakened, for he had fought Timber and a full-grown moose in little more than a day and had suffered wounds from both battles. He stumbled backwards, blood dripping into his eyes from a cut on his forehead, as another wolf menacingly walked toward him. Maya, separated from Glen and Timber, was forced to retreat up the left hill away from them entirely on her own. With Wrath and Rapid's adversaries gradually separating them, the Copperleaf would soon be fighting singly—a dangerous prospect when outnumbered.

Greymane knew that in order to defeat the Copperleaf, Wrath and Timber must be dealt with. Therefore he and his two attendants advanced upon Wrath, already fighting, and the big grey wolf was pulled down amongst four foes. Yet he was the fiercest warrior of all, and when enraged his teeth could rend an opponent apart in seconds. The other wolves, all engaged, could do nothing but watch as the four Frostwind wolves dove in, completely obscuring Wrath from view. Soon, however, the grey wolf burst forth from between them, dragging one of Greymane's dead lackeys by the throat. "Quickly!" Wrath called, barking to the other wolves. "Advance up the hill to Maya! Rapid, go to the den, and tell Paloke and Coast they must escape. We shall hold the line here." Rapid broke free and ran, living up to his name, and none of the Frostwind could follow him for his speed.

Rapid made it to the den in a matter of moments, his coat torn from the fighting. Coast and Paloke knew in a moment what had happened, for he was bathed in the Frostwind's scent. Panting heavily and nearly exhausted, the quick wolf accompanied his sister and mother as they made their way southwest, as fast and as far from Greymane's realm as possible.

The battle against Greymane's forces was long and arduous, and many brave deeds were done that day. In all, the Copperleaf slew four of Greymane's wolves, though Salyr and Wrath were badly injured. They knew Greymane's mind, and that he would seek vengeance upon them if they stayed at their old den. Paloke's pups would never be safe; they would be carried away at the earliest opportunity, to be slain or adopted into the Frostwind's ranks. Yet Greymane had done the Copperleaf a great service by driving them away, for the men from the Research Center knew the general location of their old den and would certainly search for them there.

The mountain town of Dolsty was quite unremarkable. Its economy relied mainly upon agriculture, ranching, and logging. The people there worked hard and lived good, easy lives, and were often to be found in the cold winter months in front of their fireplaces, or during the summer on their porch stoops. They told tales of two-hundred-pound wolves and eighty-pound bass, exaggerating their exploits until, as the town's saying went, "there wasn't enough truth to be squeezed out to fill a cup." Every man knew a tall tale when he heard one, and every man tolerated it with a smile or a laugh, because he knew his stories were no different.

Yet these kind folk, good enough to their fellows, had hard hearts where wolves were concerned. They were suspicious, filled with the fear founded upon old myths and superstitions, and didn't trust the wolf where their cattle were concerned. Public support for the wolf population was slim, and many wanted the animals gone from the mountains entirely: gone, and forgotten. Let the suburban animal lovers keep wolves in their backyards if they wanted; it was not their livelihood that was at stake.

This attitude had facilitated the growth of the lab into its anti-wolf research, and Haxler was only too happy to oblige the prejudices of the ranchers. He had enjoyed the defeated look in the wolves' eyes, the way some cowered as he would enter the pen and drag another into the lab, only to return it bearing a new scar, and perhaps, a new horrifying memory.

He had not meant for that defeated look ever to disappear. Nor had he meant for them to stop cowering.

But they had.

The big black wolf's lunge through the window had struck Haxler full in the chest, sending him flying across the lab. The wolf was right to conclude that he was dead, for he had lain there a long time before Barnes found him, still collapsed in the same position. He had finally awoken, simply to meet a whole new world of pain.

He was badly bruised and beaten, and several of his bones had been cracked. He had a few terrible gashes where lab equipment, cages, and broken glass had slashed his skin. Far, far worse, however, he had lost his legs; they had been shattered by the impact beyond repair.

They were gone. The black wolf had taken them away. Wolves, in general, had taken his legs. Haxler would not—could not—soon forget it. He was reminded of it every time he looked down to his lap, or what was left of it.

He had traveled to one of the big cities to get prosthetics, and was still in the process of getting used to them. But walking was now a chore. It was a means to an end, a very particular end—the Copperleaf Pack's.

Chapter Five

The Copperleaf collected themselves many miles from the old den, far too tired to care whether the Frostwind had pursued them. All, with the exception of Paloke, were wounded to some extent. They looked to one another with mournful eyes, and Coast tended to their wounds as best she could, though some, like Salyr, were quite badly off. Greymane's forces had done their work but it was doubtful that they would follow the Copperleaf far outside their own boundaries, for their concern was maintaining their territory. The pack had to think of where they would go next, for they were again homeless.

Salyr thought long and hard before he reached a solution. "I believe I've got the perfect place to live. It's in the far northwest, near Washbourne Falls. It will be a long journey of many miles, but I think we can make it. We will have to cross several roads"—a sharp intake of breath met this admission—"but quite few. It is past the Barren Lands, where men have cleared the forest, and there is no reason for them to go there any more. A massive fir tree stands there, its roots nestling a hole in the ground. It would make a wonderful den. The puppies could frolic about the vast fields which lie in front of it. You can see all around you, though a large hill rests to one side. How does it sound?"

Glen closed his eyes for a moment, then turned to Paloke. "Can you envision such a place to raise our cubs?" he asked.

"It sounds wonderful," Paloke said. "But things that sound so fair may quickly go awry."

"You needn't be such a pessimist, mother!" admonished Rapid. "How many days will the journey take us, Salyr?"

The dog was laying on his stomach, one eye closed, a large cut just above it. His body was slashed through entirely, and his breaths were long and labored. "Far too many, if we go on like this. We should stay here a few days and simply rest, even though we are fairly close to a road. Most of us have gorged ourselves on the calf, so we needn't worry about food. If we travel as quickly as we can, we should be there in three days' time."

Glen whined contentedly. "It is good. We will leave in several days. Rest yourselves, my children, and perhaps our journey will come to an end, and we shall be safe again."

⁂

Rapid whined uneasily. It was early in the morning, and the town was for the most part not awake yet, but the sun was up eighteen hours a day now. The thin wolf blinked back the sunlight which was coming down far too brightly through the firs. He was more worried, however, by the road which lay just beyond them. It smelt of car oil, tar, and the soured scent of all man-things left to waste. But worst of all, it smelt of Death. A badger lay on its side, striped head tilted at an unnatural angle, its face a grim caricature of alarm. It had been there for some time, and would remain so—the road was not well-known, and led only to a small lake, and, passing that, some farmland and the lab.

It was the second day of the wolves' trek, to be by far the longest, for they were going through men's territory and would be unsafe much of the time. They had just begun, and Salyr stood confidently upon the road, calling to the wolves, who stood hesitantly to the side, watching uncertainly.

"Come on, then!" prompted Salyr. "At this rate we'll not get far. You'll never get past the bridge if you can't do this. There hasn't been anyone along here for at least two days, and the road itself isn't going to leap up and swallow you!"

As if the mere suggestion of such an incident could make it occur, Timber, whose paw was almost upon the road, pulled it back quickly. Glen, standing around his troupe, looked up at the dog. "It's very easy for you to say. They won't shoot you the moment they lay eyes on you. And what about that badger? I suppose it died like that on its own?"

"What nonsense. It's the cars that come by. You know what they are, you've seen them before, though you don't know the word. The big metal beasts which make loud growling noises. The men sit in their stomachs and get taken places faster. Another *teyen*, I suppose." Some of the wolves smiled inwardly at this comment, for Salyr used it with almost as much contempt as the pack themselves.

"Cars aren't really dangerous, unless you look in their eyes. The eyes don't take in light at night—they give it off, and it blinds you. But canines have more sense than to get trapped; its only the smaller creatures and the hunted ones, like deer, that stop when they can't see. The cars almost never halt, except when the men tell them to, so if the men don't see the animal in front, or don't care, the car will just keep on going, and trample it to death. That's what happened to the badger, and that is almost the only danger on a road."

"Except if a man with a gun is walking down it," added Paloke apprehensively. "Still, I think I understand cars now. They seem quite stupid. No wonder they allow men to climb into their stomachs and order them around without getting fed up and eating them." The other wolves murmured in agreement, but they still stayed in the sand on the side of the road, watching Salyr intently.

"It's all very good if you understand cars now, but what next should I explain to persuade you to cross? Perhaps through the very act of reciting the history of the world while I stand in the middle of this road, I may convince you to cross. You may then decide, thinking the better of it, that it would be more prudent to wait until the world is finished in its entirety and there isn't any history left to be written, so that you may better plan how to go about crossing the next few feet. Therefore I shall begin with how the *Aynsen* first created the soil and the plants, and the first deer which learned that he must eat the plants in order to survive –"

Timber, grumbling, hopped up onto the road, stepping gingerly as if it offended his paws. "Point taken, Salyr, and I shall cross, if only to get you to shut your mouth." The enormous wolf's nose twitched, sniffing the road curiously. He looked up and down its length, seeing if the morning shadows concealed a hidden foe. "It is good," he barked shortly, and though he detested staying upon the road, he waited until the entire pack had made their way to the other side before he crossed himself.

"Excellent," said Salyr. "There's a lake not far from here. We'll go there and get a drink, and follow the stream that feeds it for several miles. That will take most of the day at our pace, I'm afraid, though small game is plentiful along the banks. By evening we should arrive at the bridge: a road over the water, so the cars don't get wet. I've heard they don't like it; water ruins their coat. We'll spend the night after we get through the Barren Lands. We should be safe enough there. Half of it used to be forest last year, if you fellows ever bothered to go that far west. But more men have come into the town lately, and they need somewhere to live. They felled the forest and have made many new homes with the trunks, even sending some away—'lumber', they call it—and all that is left there are grass and stumps, for miles upon miles."

"This land is bleak," said Glen. "Men have changed it much since last summer. I do not remember this 'bridge,' nor do I recall any expanse of forest devastation so vast as to be called the Barren Lands."

"Yes, they have changed much, and all, so it seems, for the worse," said Rapid. "Men do very little which is not for their own gain, nor do they think ahead. What will they do when they have cleared all these forests? When there is no more wood with which to build? When the animals have left this valley and they starve?"

"It is not as simple as all that," commented Salyr. "Men are everywhere, in greater numbers than you can imagine. They all work in a great web. If no living creatures stirred among these mountains other than humans, still other men would come, bearing meat for them, and they would be no worse off. The only time they will realize that they have nothing left is when the whole world becomes the Barren Lands."

The wolves were disconcerted by this prospect. Rapid and Coast, who especially took joy in regarding nature, were deeply saddened, and as the pack marched along they cast their eyes on each flower and each insect in turn, weeping for it. The Copperleaf were silent for several hours as they kept up their steady trot, only pausing every now and then to lap up the cool stream water or to listen for some phantom sound of men.

Finally, the lop-eared dog turned to address the rest of the pack. They had stopped under the bright green glint of pin cherry trees in the afternoon sun. "It's rough going from here, I'm afraid, and we won't be entirely safe until tomorrow afternoon. We're in human country, and its all open land. Look beyond."

The wolves regarded their surroundings. The pin cherries marked the end of the forest, for beyond them were softly swaying grasses. To their left they could see distant wooden posts for wire fences, behind which cattle grazed in mute ignorance. A wide, winding dirt path cut through the dull green, leading up to Salyr's 'bridge' on the right, which crossed their stream. The road quickly dissolved past the bridge, for all was dirt there—dirt, mud, and weeds, and amongst them the stumps of thousands of dead trees. The void carried up as far as they could see, over the hill. "It is a sad sight," whispered Coast.

"Yet we must pass through it," answered Salyr regretfully.

"Quickly, we must cross the bridge before men come. The wind tells of none for miles, but we wish to be far into the Barren Lands before any arrive."

Wolves adapt quickly to new situations, being intelligent animals, and having once crossed a road, the bridge was hardly more difficult. Maya had scurried back into the bushes as the wooden slats creaked beneath her paws, and it was a while before she believed that the bridge had not growled at her.

The air was rank with the smell of old sap and burnt wood as the pack trekked through the Barren Lands. There was no sign of new tree growth to be seen. No birds stirred, for there was nowhere for them to perch except amidst the sparse clumps of high grasses. Deer mice and meadow voles, disoriented, scurried underneath the wolves' feet, and Maya, still full of pup-like curiosity due to her time in the lab, nipped at them playfully. Once the pack noticed a red fox hunting rodents among the tree stumps, but anything larger had learned to avoid the Barren Lands. Men would often come to cut trees, but if they saw a coat that they liked, they did not hesitate to take it home. Seven wolves walking single-file through the lonely landscape would have made a better photograph than a rug, but had a man been there to choose, even though they weren't in winter coat, the pack probably would have adorned a hearth.

At last, as they made it over a particularly desolate hilltop, where only a raven rested its tired wings, the pack came upon a welcome sight. Amongst the deer grass stood several mountain ashes, rich with small white flowers and dotted with sparks of berries. Beyond them, to either side, were vast stretches of white spruce, proof that the logging industry had not come this far in.

"This is beautiful country," admitted Timber, careful not to look at the desolation behind him.

"If we make it down to the mountain-ash we can sleep out the rest of the afternoon," said Salyr. "Start again when the moon is high and everyone is rested, and we should make it to the new densite by daybreak. I didn't expect that we'd keep this pace, with all our wounds. After we heal ourselves, we should be able to make it from the bridge to the den in a quarter of a day." It was evident that the day's journey had weighed heavily upon the young dog, and several of his cuts had begun to open up and bleed again.

"There . . . aren't any other packs here, are there?" asked Coast cautiously, her white forepaw held high, still in its cast. "I should think we've had enough trouble."

"Surprisingly, there aren't. There are some coyotes about, but they mostly cause trouble at the ranches farther southwest. And we can deal with a band of them, should the need arise."

The wolves showed their approval, then all marched down to the tiny copse of mountain ash, availing themselves of the berries. They slept serenely, for they had crossed many miles that day, and all were weary.

Soundlessly they roused themselves at nightfall, knowing that it was time to continue. The night life was quite different, and dark-coated deer watched them warily from their beds and dinners in the thickets while several coyotes chased smaller animals. The wolves quickly entered the safety and sanctity of the forest, and beneath the cover of the trees they were finally at ease.

At last they arrived, slightly before sunrise. Above them towered a majestic alpine fir, with so many branches that they could not perceive its end. Some of its lowest branches, weighted down in winter with snow, had taken root. There was a hole to the side of it, a burrow or natural cave of some sort, and as the wolves stuck their heads in one at a time, they noted that the roof of the underground tunnel was held up by the roots. Paloke regarded it for some time.

"Is it fitting?" Glen asked his mate.

"It should be. I need to expand it somewhat, and dig out the back, what with three pups on the way. One's been using his legs quite a bit. It looks like Rapid is going to have some competition." The black wolf trotted in place, embarrassed. "Digging it out won't take any time at all, however. The soil is quite soft."

Glen looked about them. "The territory will be fruitful, there is a lot of game about. I'm only worried about the blind spot. We can see into the field, and we can escape behind us. But what's to stop men from coming over the hills on either side? If they are downwind, they'll have the view of a bird, and will be able to slay several of us before we can disappear within the forest."

"The north flank is taken care of; it leads to a steep cliff. The way we came down is the only one left unguarded," said Salyr.

"Unfortunately, that's the town side," said Glen. "I suppose we'll just have to be careful, perhaps post sentries when the winds tell us to. The position we were in wasn't any better."

"Ah, the sun is rising," mentioned Salyr, catching the glint upon the leaves above. "There is a sight I must show you. Come." With that he lead them up the hill to the cliff. Far-off mountains shone as the sun rose above them, casting an orange glow about them which radiated even onto the wolves' fur. "Beautiful, is it not?" asked the lop-eared dog.

"It is amazing," Coast said breathlessly. "We have had such little beauty in our lives since Haxler." The others agreed, and all regarded the scene in mute wonder.

"Then let us hope," Salyr said kindly, "That your lives shall now be filled with it, until the end of your days."

Chapter Six

The pack had lived in the new den eleven days before the birthing began. Typically in a wolf pack, the time of birth is private, for the female alone. She must make the journey by herself, and none may help her. Never before had Glen intruded; yet he sensed that Paloke was in trouble. He had worried about her, for he had noticed on their wanderings that Paloke was sorely weighted by the pups and quite unwell. She was getting old and had survived the rigors of the lab, and Glen could not help but wonder if this final trial would be too much for her.

As time dragged by, Paloke seemed in pain. She whined loudly, much to the distress of those outside, especially Glen. The *tanah* finally ducked into the den, whining with his mate and trying to find out what was wrong. "You have never been in pain before," said Glen frantically, pacing back and forth, his ears tucked back against his head. "Why is this happening?"

Glen found one pup, its paws flailing helplessly, on the dirt in front of Paloke. The *maisa*'s eyes were shut tight against the pain and she made no response to Glen. He noticed that the afterbirth had not been cleaned off the pup and it was suffering. Wasting no time, he licked the pup clean, and the little female uttered a short gasp.

Glen was unsure what to do, for he had never been present for a birthing, and he had a sense that he shouldn't be here. Yet despite his discomfort he encouraged Paloke, coaxing her along to remain conscious. Eventually, Paloke gave birth to a second pup, a son. Again Glen cleaned the pup for her. Though the pup had not been born a moment before, it threw a sharp kick to Glen's forehead as he cleaned it. This one would be strong. At that moment Glen named him Sprint. He remembered one other pup with legs as strong as drawn timber; Rapid had been that one.

Yet Paloke was still suffering.

Glen waited. He watched his mate's face anxiously. Her mouth bent back into a grimace and her eyes were shut so tightly Glen wondered if they would ever open again.

Nothing happened. Paloke's muscles relaxed in utter exhaustion.

"I can't do it, Glen. I'll die if I try," she whispered, her eyelids opening a slit.

"No you won't. You'll die if you don't try. The last pup…it's relying upon you. We must bring it into the world, so that it may roam among the trees and hunt the great elk. Try, please," he begged. The air in the small den seemed oppressive and cramped, hot with emotion and strain. Glen, the majestic *tanah*, for the first time in his life genuinely scared, tucked his tail between his legs and arched his back, cowering in fear of his mate's life. "You must do this, Paloke!

You must!"

With a mighty heave Paloke gave birth to the last pup.

"Thank you," Glen whispered, moving toward the motionless pup. He whined softly, licking it. It lay in an odd position, and the Death smell began to waft from it. Glen regarded it in pain. Even after the trials of the wilderness and the horrors of the lab, nothing in his life had ever been so painful. The sight of the blank little eyes, now never to see the world, seemed to grip his stomach and twist it viciously. The pup's fur was dark grey, a tiny star of white painted across the chest. Glen spoke to the dead pup, summoning all the emotions he felt at the moment, all the strife that lay within him. "I'm sorry. I'm sorry that you will never see the massive expanses of the basins, the endless snow tundra of the north, the forests that expand forever. I'm sorry that you can never know the thrill of the chase, the pure joy of running through the snow, the blood of the hunt coursing through your body. I'm sorry that you can't imagine the world you left behind, and how rich, how endlessly vast it is."

Glen paused, watching the little body mournfully, vainly hoping to detect some sign of life, if even for an instant. "Let me try to paint you a picture. Endless blue skies, spreading over our heads, above our reach. The trees endeavor to touch those skies, their rich, green leaves spreading out in all directions, yearning to embrace the clouds. And perhaps some do.

"Reaching higher into the sky are the mountains, beyond the meadows and the forests, the tops of their crags lost in the mists. They say that hidden among those mists are the *Aynsen*, our angels. They also say that with the *Aynsen* are our departed, watching the pack from their vantage point on the peaks. Perhaps that is where you are, my son." Glen's head hung low.

Rapid burst through the entrance, his eyes averted to the side of the den, not daring to look beyond. "I apologize for this intrusion, father, but I could not wait any longer. There is something wrong, I gather, and the Death smell is strong. What has happened?"

"Your mother is very ill. One of the puppies is dead." Rapid could not help but look at his father, wondering at his tone. He had never seen his father so distraught, a small, broken wolf, huddled at the end of the den. Glen's eyes were glassy with shock and fright, his manner almost hysterical.

Rapid left quickly, unable to bear the scene. He told the others of their mother's plight, and the Cloud Tree was soon surrounded by frantic wolves. They waited until darkness fell before Glen painfully crawled out from beneath the den. He walked straight past the semicircle of wolves, into the fields beyond, his eyes glazed in stupor. "Father!" Rapid called. The old wolf, his grizzled grey-white mane now seeming ancient, turned to face his son blankly. "What of mother?" the younger wolf asked intently.

"She . . . seems much better. No happiness tonight. We will hold a ceremony for the dead pup." He turned again to disappear into the fields.

"Father!" the cry echoed again. This time it was Timber, and Glen greeted him with the same blank stare. "How many pups?"

"Two," said Glen with a weak smile. And though the others worried for Glen, they rejoiced at the news. Their pack would be larger, and when one of them became *tanah*, he would rule over these young ones at a time when they would be in their prime.

That night, during the ceremony, Paloke lay close to the dead pup, huddled in a ball, her tail tucked over her back and down along her cheek, passing over her nose so as to hide her face like a veil. Sickness emanated from her, and she seemed barely conscious, and then only in quiet pain.

When a pup died, all else, even the sickness of the mother, had to be put away for a time. One by one, starting with Paloke and Glen and ending with Wrath, the pack curled up with sadness next to the tiny pup they never knew, paying their respects with silent resolution.

Paloke could not stay with her departed young one, and eventually left, with a final sad nuzzle, to tend to his littermates. The rest of the wolves had to stay throughout the night with the pup, and in the morning it would be buried*. A leaf fell on Maya's head from above. She did not move it.

Five weeks passed since the pups were born, and both had developed distinct personalities. Their bodies were quickly maturing, though the huge paws and knobby knees of youth that foretold growth yet to come were still present. They were able to accompany the older wolves on forays into the forest of up to a mile's distance.

Sprint was, as both Glen and Paloke had predicted, full of strength and vigor, clearly dominant over his sister. His feet took him far afield in search of new play places, and he was quick enough to bring down a hare with only his milk teeth at four weeks, though

---

* Wolves have been noted to bury dead pups, both in the wild and in captivity.

he was unable to eat it until Coast had regurgitated it for him. Sprint's manner was always playful, and his wit was as quick as his feet, though he had not mastered either yet.

Crystal, as Sprint's littermate was called, was far smaller than her grey brother, though of the same markings. She hovered about Paloke constantly, seldom venturing out of her mother's shadow. She was not a coward, simply quieter, more of a watcher than her brother.

While there had been an unusual warm weather streak during their escape, a brief cold front had followed, during which snow could be seen upon the mountain-tops. The weather was returning to its earlier warmth just as quickly, and the wolves were unsettled as to what the erratic conditions would mean.

Paloke had been hard-hit by the cold weather. She had never recovered from the difficult birthing, and it seemed that the life ebbed out of her even as it grew in the pups. Though the pack could not have known, or fully understood, Paloke was in her tenth year, far too old to carry on as she did. She was taken to resting the days away, and hardly ever hunted with the others. They brought as much meat back to her as they could, but they were filled with worry. How would she survive, if game proved scarce in the fall?

The pack was plagued with thoughts of Haxler. Timber was tortured by his last images of the man, flying across the test table, collapsed and bloody in the corner with the dogs crying out in horror and excitement. Often on long trips, or when they were resting, the wolves would turn and nudge the scars on their tails, as if trying to free themselves from something that lay there. They knew that all was not right.

The wolves left Paloke on a hunt somewhat reluctantly, because the old *maisa* seemed especially devoid of strength that day. She lay huddled underground with an air that told the others not to approach her. As soon as she could sense their hesitation, she acted well, bidding them goodbye as they left. Afterward she collapsed, exhausted and out of breath. The two pups crowded around her, unable to understand what was happening.

The Copperleaf did not kill that day. They found an elk that had died of natural causes. It seemed to have been dead for some time, for the carcass had been ravaged by lesser animals.

Glen left the carcass speedily. The old male sensed that something was amiss. Rapid started to follow, but lagged behind. His father was traveling faster than he had ever seen, and even Rapid could not outpace the old warrior. Glen rushed into the den, his eyes filling with sadness. The smell of Death was beginning to burn through Paloke's body. The two pups whined in confusion.

Glen rushed toward his beloved mate. "Paloke?" he whispered gently.

Her right ear twitched, ever so slightly, in a feeble attempt to respond.

Glen sighed with relief, trying not to sound disturbed. The sight of his mate like this bit deep into his soul. He cringed inwardly. "Good, you can still hear me. You can pull through this. Do it for the pups," he spoke softly. He felt that the slightest pressure might blow Paloke away into the wind, like a brittle autumn leaf.

The Death smell faded for an instant. As if from the dead,

Paloke's breath carried with it her parting words. "I have given them all I have to offer. The rest of the pack may care for them now. Only through dying can I help the Copperleaf, by freeing them of my burden. Take care, Glen, to remember that no being is eternal, though the ages that we have lived seem to challenge that. We would be better to pass our strength to our youth, who hold a stronger flicker of that younger life which you try so hard to grasp. The truth is, Glen, that the flame of your youth has waned away, and you can only keep it bright so long until, at last, you are too tired to maintain it. Pass it on before it disappears, for otherwise it shall do good to none."

Paloke moved no more, and as the rest of the pack returned to the densite, they bowed their heads in turn. Out of the little hole beneath the Cloud Tree, the Death scent billowed.

Chapter Seven

No play came to the wolf pack for a long time. A week passed and Glen dutifully found a rendezvous site for the pups to frolic not far from Cloud Tree. He sought solace in attending to the pups' needs, but no joy remained in his eyes—only the old warrior strength, the determination to see the hunt to its end, was still there. He could not believe that now, after spending most of his life with the old grey wolf, she was gone. The whole pack was saddened, but they all knew that life went on, and there was no use holding on to the painful past in the face of a bright future.

It was said that Coast would make a good, caring mother. The instinct was strong, and Paloke had appointed Coast as mother to the pups for the times she had gone hunting. Now that Paloke was dead, Coast became their adoptive mother. Rapid watched the pups also, and seemed to enjoy putting his paw over their backs and stroking them gently. It was said he would make a good father.

Paloke's death had weighed heavily on Salyr's mind, and for

several days he left the pack, wandering across the vast expanse of fields until he reached the eastern forest. He traveled for a time upon its soil, deep in thought, until he happened upon a small meadow. He was surprised by it, for below the meadow was a large barn with a dirt pen by its side. As he neared, he could not mistake the scent, though old, of the Copperleaf. Dogs yelped and howled from within the barn, and Salyr listened in shock to their tortured cries, for they were his kin, and he could imagine their pains as they lamented them. The lights were on within, and two men worked there, though their silhouettes only showed in one window. The other window was boarded up, for it had been broken. Salyr fell to the ground, struck by the realization that he had happened upon the lab which had committed such evils to the Copperleaf.

While Salyr lay, stunned, among the wildflowers, he was able to separate the haze of smells emanating from the lab. One stood out in particular, as Wrath had described it in detail. It smelt of maskingly clean chemicals, of pollution, and of short temper. Oddly enough, Salyr could not smell many of the usual human scents on this man, as if he had covered them up or they had never been. There was not a doubt in his mind that this was Haxler, that he had returned and was readying more tests for new wolves. As Salyr rose to leave, the door to the lab opened, and Haxler appeared, heavy with the Death scent, a small dog slung limply over his shoulder. He was chatting to the man inside as he threw his load into a nearby ditch in the forest. Salyr caught only a few key words that he had learned while living amongst humans, among them 'town,' 'cattle,' and 'wolves.' What was going to happen at town? And did it have something to do with the wolves?

Salyr darted back into the forest, then continued back to Cloud Tree in haste. He knew what he must do.

⌘

Coast and Salyr were walking the pups about the rendezvous site, watching as they darted over logs and around trees. Crystal seized a piece of deer hide from an old hunt and tossed it playfully over her head, and Sprint darted over her to get it, tumbling them both into the ground, where they scuffled with mock ferocity.

So far the two caretakers had kept to idle chatter in the warm evening breeze, yet Coast could tell that Salyr's mind was burdened and he wished to talk to her. "What's wrong, Salyr?"

Salyr swallowed, returning her stare. "I think I'm going to leave the pack. At least for a while. I didn't talk to Wrath because I knew he'd try to change my mind."

Coast turned away, looking up through the spiraling branches of a fir tree. Salyr nosed a pine cone. "Why?" she asked earnestly. "Are you tired of our life here?" 'After all,' she thought privately, '*He's just a dog. Life out here for a day or two would be extremely strenuous, yet he's done it for nearly half a season.*'

"Your life is hard here, I can deal with that. There may be trouble in town, though, and I think it has to do with you wolves. I may be able to help you. I'll be able to make visits, but I can't live with you here, at least for some time. Until things calm down, it'll be too dangerous, and I may lead them to you. I think you should move far, far north, where these people can no longer hunt you and torture you. Do it now."

Coast did not understand him, for his words were far more serious than as was his wont, and she could see they were a portent of things to come. "Tell me more, Salyr," she pleaded searchingly. The breeze lightly ruffled her pure white fur. "We can't move now, not with the pups so young. What's going on?"

At last he told her that Haxler was alive, and he had seen and smelled him. The dog was deeply troubled as he saw the pain and worry in Coast's eyes, a look he had not seen for a long while. "Do what you can to keep the pups safe," the dog said, raising himself up to leave. "If he comes and takes you back, keep them hidden. He does not know about them yet. I shall care for them, and raise them in the ways of the wild, if all else fails." With that, the dog hurried over the fields and toward the town.

While the two adults talked, the pups wandered away in the evening light to the cliffside Salyr had dubbed the Lookout Point. Their path wound about continually, as it is the habit of all young animals to wish to investigate the unknown, and the world was yet new to them.

Both pairs of bright blue eyes fixed upon the moon, which cast an odd purple mist over the cliff top. The brother and sister were quiet for a long time, though they sensed each other's feelings as close siblings often can.

Crystal's silk-like hairs caught upon a bramble bush as she studied it, and she tugged until she tore free, giving it a puzzled, backward glance as if puzzled why the bush would wish to stick to her. The young pup was growing at a rate that indicated she would be smaller than the rest of the Copperleaf, even Maya, but what she lacked in size she made up for in beauty. Her coat was long and luxuriant, even for a five-week-old, her eyes thoughtful and serene, her fangs long and sharp. She had a small, pretty snout highlighted down the middle with a streak of dark russet.

"What are you thinking about?" Crystal asked, nibbling at a burr that had caught between her guard hairs. She could guess where his mind was, for it had been fixated upon the same subject for several days. Sprint remained silent, though, watching the far-off mountain tops until they disappeared into the clouds. His tail gently wagged, telling her that he was glad to have her company, but he gave no other sign. Crystal was puzzled, for Sprint had never denied her a response. She cleaned her paws and waited.

"Why did our brother die before he was born? Sometimes I wonder what it would be like if he had lived with us," Sprint said at last.

"He was my twin," Crystal offered, but she knew it brought him little insight. She was perplexed by his questions and did not know how to properly answer them. To her they had no bearing on the present, and therefore no reason to be asked. It was not for them to dwell upon these matters, but to play amongst the high grasses, to beg for food, to sleep in the underground warmth of the den. Yet this was the question that Sprint had asked every night for far too long.

"Why did mother abandon us? We needed her, but she died. Even father asked her to stay for us, but she wouldn't listen," Sprint continued. His manner carried a note of frustration.

"Rapid said it was time for her to go with the *Aynsen*, and she could not refuse their call," Crystal answered, the same way she had responded for several nights.

Sprint pushed some pebbles off the cliff, then watched them tumble down the treacherous scarp. "You know I'm not satisfied with that answer," Sprint said sulkily.

"I know," Crystal admitted. "But you'll have to be," she said, turning to go. "None of us have any better ones."

The small herd of mule deer grazed among the firs and aspens, chewing the succulent grasses contentedly. Four seasoned warriors watched them from the safety of the forest, splitting into groups of two, conversing on what approach they should take. This was the work of wolves; this was their livelihood.

Rapid and Timber worked along one side, quietly acknowledging with Wrath and Glen their part in the hunt, though it was never discussed. They would be the first to break cover, to select the prey. Theirs was not to kill the animal, but to mark it for the others.

The two black wolves came out into the open, breaking formation in a slow trot, Rapid in the lead. The herd watched, startled, as the wolves moved ever closer. They could sense that this was a hunt. As Rapid seemed ready to pass away from the deer, he broke his trot and charged at a doe, baring his fangs but not attacking.

Wrath and Glen did not come to his aid.

Nor were they meant to. Rapid had not marked the doe, for she was in her prime, but had attacked her to distract a huge male which lorded over the herd. As he did so, Timber caught up to the herd, heading for the pack's target, a little fawn. He let out a high-pitched whine, marking the fawn for others to attack.

Wrath and Glen burst out from the brush, leaping into the fray, while Timber helped Rapid draw the stag away. Wrath leapt upon the fawn, tumbling it to the ground with zeal. Glen's jaws opened, and the animal's fate seemed sealed.

Rapid and Timber, however, had not expected the buck to be so combative, for they had smelled sickness upon him. He sent Rapid fleeing into the woods and aimed a vicious kick at Timber's skull. The big wolf barely managed to deflect the blow, but the impact still sent him sprawling. He lay stunned on the ground, barely conscious, his tongue hanging from slack jaws.

Wrath leaped away from the fawn. In the back of his mind he could tell that the hunt had reawakened his joint pains, but he could not heed them now. Timber was at the mercy of the stag, which was poised to trample him to death. Wrath, whom the other wolves had always viewed as selfish, was in a position to make the ultimate sacrifice, for he was the only one close enough to turn the stag's attention away from Timber. By leaping at the male deer in his present state, his joints thundering, Wrath knew he would close his fate. Yet Timber was his brother, his littermate, and perhaps by saving him he could atone for his failure in saving Tundra.

The big grey wolf winced with pain, begging his body to carry through this one last action. As he charged forward, he turned his whine into a roar, leaping for the stag's throat. But he had not been quick enough, and the buck turned his head, his antlers about to catch Wrath in the chest. The wolf tried to swing away, but in the throes of his agony, all he could do was flail his legs helplessly. He saw the massive head turn, saw the huge antlers approaching swiftly . . . He closed his eyes, forming his mouth into a grimace. '*Tundra!*' he thought frantically as his dead brother's image flashed through his mind. '*I'm coming, brother. . . .*'

The antlers struck Wrath full in the chest, shattering his ribs and tossing him aside like a leaf. He struck the ground with a sickly thud, coughing blood before collapsing, with glazed eyes, into the flowers. Timber, with a cry of anguish, pulled up to catch the buck's neck. The buck fell to the forest floor, its blood spouting freely upon the grasses it had grazed upon a moment before.

The other deer, including the little fawn, ran to the safety of a thicket. A slight rustling, then silence. Glen stood agape, despair swelling within him. The wind tossed gentle leaves to the ground in whispers as the breeze gently caressed the wolves' fur. They stood motionless, each regarding the other. Blood still flowed from the buck's fatal wound. Wrath's body lay crumpled among the flowers beneath a tall aspen.

Whimpering, Timber approached his brother's body. Wrath's eyes blinked, and for a moment the black wolf took hope, licking his brother's muzzle gently.

Wrath's golden eyes blinked no more.

Rapid stepped beside Timber, then lay with his heart to the soil. He put one paw on his departed brother's chest. The clearing was deathly silent. Glen reached over and nuzzled his fallen son's ear with his cheek.

Presently, when the warm breeze had ceased and even the grasses lay still, Rapid and Glen rose and moved out of the clearing. Timber remained. Alone.

※

Night fell, and Timber watched the sky. Wolves don't name the constellations, but nonetheless he regarded the stars and found them familiar. The buck, uneaten, lay across from Timber in the clearing. The scene looked peaceful, yet there were signs of the violence that had befallen the quiet meadow. Timber had not left Wrath's side since his death.

It was getting more difficult to fend off other prying beasts, for they eyed the wolf's body greedily. Some had fed upon the buck, but many wished to see what prize a wolf so large as Timber might be guarding so fiercely.

After Timber had driven away a hawk, a voice called from across the clearing. "Look at you, Timber. Your littermate knew what he was getting into when he jumped. He saved you because he loved you. You can't repay him now, by staying here. He is dead. There is nothing left to do." The voice was Salyr's. "Rapid caught up with me, and I came as quickly as I heard. Luckily I was spying upon the men in the Barren Lands, and not far from here. I don't have long before I should head to town—ask the others why—but I'd like to help you if I can, despite the tension between us."

Timber stared at the dog a while, before commenting gruffly, "Earth knows how long you've been downwind, watching me. Well, what do you want?"

The dog strode up to the body. "I wished to pay my respects to your brother. He was my first friend here. I owe him so much. And

I feel as if I could have saved him, were I with you. If only I had waited to leave but one day, I would have been here." He motioned to Wrath.

"Think of it this way, Timber. If he had nothing to repay you for, he would not have sacrificed his life for you. Even if all you ever granted him was a grudging, brotherly bond, he deemed that enough to end his own life for you. Judging by what I've heard, I suppose his joint pains acted up, so that he could not dodge the buck."

Timber's eyes softened. "If I had but known, I would have warned him, would have kept him from hunting the big animals."

Salyr shook his head. "It is the job of men to live upon 'ifs', not ours. We both must put them aside, though they bear down upon us greatly. Besides, Wrath wouldn't have wanted to live that way. He enjoyed the hunt too much.

"Wrath was his own master. He was the type of wolf that takes care of himself, strikes out on his own."

Timber regarded the lop-eared dog solemnly. "Then why didn't he?"

"Perhaps . . . he knew the pack needed him," answered Salyr, a slight smile on his face.

Chapter Eight

The Research Center that still tortured the Copperleaf in their dreams remained in operation. Haxler and Barnes were continually receiving and fulfilling new contracts from clients, contracts that kept them testing drugs and chemicals on the myriad number of dogs that passed but once through their doors. Yet the wolves were not forgotten; the anti-wolf ranchers and their partners often requested progress reports on the wolf experiments, while Haxler pleaded delay based upon his recovery from his injuries. None outside of the lab knew that the wolves had escaped, but the scientists could no longer put off telling the public about the incident.

"Well, look here," stuttered Barnes. "They shouldn't become too excited if we tell them the wolves escaped. I mean, the odds of them actually being dangerous to men. . . ."

The young vet halted uncertainly, his eyes downcast, as Haxler glared coldly. Beneath Haxler's eyes the skin had grown hollow and dark, as if he never slept. His hair had become gray and dull, his flesh sallow. Recovering from his ordeal with Timber had left him spent, and he looked far older than the man of forty-some years that he was. Barnes had noted that his employer's mood had grown grim and ominous, his actions with the dogs far more extreme and unmerciful. It seemed as if he had grown a streak of sadism with regard to anything that walked on four feet. "They've already proven they are dangerous to us. Look what they've done, Jon! *Look!*" He pointed angrily at the prosthetics. Then he drew inward, thinking to himself, as was often his habit these days. "Even if we hide that they've done this, the fools will panic. I mean, imagine how much they feared the damned wolves before the wolves had done anything to them! Their imaginations will join with their ignorance the moment we release the information. Wolves from a testing lab! Genetic mutations out for revenge! To slaughter their children and their cattle! That's how it will go. And once they've done the wolves in, the blame will fall on us. Yes, us, Jon. We'll be put in the sighters, too. Never mind that we were trying to make their world safer."

Barnes ground his teeth inwardly. "If they'll panic, wouldn't it be safer just to capture another pack, and act like nothing's happened?"

"That wouldn't do. Those were the ones with the CDLs, and that's our biggest commission, remember that. What would we say to that wolf hybrid breeder if we told him we've lost all our prototypes? He'd join the rest in skinning us, surely."

Jon was tiring of this debate. He had to agree with Haxler that they needed to save their own skins, but he wished that they could break free of the necessity to do so. '*If the whole business wasn't covered in sin,*' he thought as he looked about the room at the newest batch of victims, '*Perhaps we wouldn't need to watch our backs so often. But there's no way to clean up an operation like this.*'

Haxler continued his thoughts. "I suppose the best way to handle it is to drive all the attention toward the wolves. Admit that they're a danger to people. They'll be killed, undoubtedly, but we'll salvage the bodies and be able to reach some weak conclusions about the CDLs' physiological effects. It's the psychological ones we're looking for, but we'll at least have the implants back so we can try again."

'*And again, and again, if needs be,*' thought Barnes bitterly. '*Try until all the wolves in these mountains are murdered. And why stop there? It won't. Not if there are people like me in the world, who don't lift a finger against this.*' Jon's head sunk to his chest, and he closed his eyes, his hand gripping the table tightly. What he was about to do would only add to his torment.

Dolsty's town hall had been a gathering place for nearly a hundred years. Haxler noted bitterly as he made his way to the podium that the building smelled like it. There was a strong musty odor, and the inside was dank and poorly lit, yet there was a warmth in the old log structure that many people found comforting.

Most of the town had responded to the notice that the "Wolf Problem" would be addressed this morning, with speeches by the two scientists who had studied the wolves and tried to end the animals' threat to the town.

It was almost a pity, in a way, that Dolsty *didn't* have any problem wolves. They do exist, though they aren't common: wolves hunt by search image, and if they haven't seen their pack members eat an animal, they won't perceive it as food, which is why most livestock are left unharmed. Yet a wolf falling upon hard times will occasionally attack a cow or sheep, and, having acquired a new search image, begin to hunt those animals as food. Fortunately for the people of Dolsty, though coyotes had infrequently slain livestock, no wolf—of the Frostwind, the Copperleaf, or the other few packs in the area—had as yet required a taste for them. The ranchers didn't seem daunted by this fact, however, and the menace was so widely talked about that the wolves may as well have killed several dozen cows.

Today in the large meeting house the air was stifling and hot with the presence of so many bodies in such limited space. One man had jokingly mentioned to Barnes that the entire town had shown up to hear them speak. Jonathan's faith in humanity sunk a little lower at the compliment.

Haxler stood tall, surveying the crowd with satisfaction. He knew the townspeople would be receptive to the dangers the wolves posed. He would get his revenge; they would bring him the body of the black male that had shattered his life. Then he would laugh at those defiant gold eyes, for they would be filled with impotent rage which meant nothing.

"Hello, everyone. I've come to discuss the wolf menace," Haxler said. He was met by loud cheers and whistles. "This is Jonathan Barnes, and he works with me down at our animal testing facility. We've been working for almost a year now to try and make your lives, your children's lives, safe from these beasts. During that time we've learned a few things I'm sure you folks already know. First, wolves can't be trusted. They'd often take a snap at one of us when we were out there, say, cleaning their pen. We'd be minding our own business, when suddenly one would take a leap at us, and it would be all we could do to get away. Second, wolves are vicious creatures, subject to a lot of in-fighting and cruel acts to other animals. Why, a few times a dog from the lab . . . er, one of our pets, got into the pen accidentally and was torn to pieces. You don't see your dogs ripping each other apart and eating each other, I'm sure. Completely different natures, wild natures. Fully capable of bringing down a bison in the wild. What does that mean they're going to do to your livestock? What's to stop them from dragging away your child in the night? For they are smart, I must admit, and they could easily sneak in an open window and grab a baby from its cradle. Now, now, I'm not trying to get you worried, just concerned. That's why I'm here, why Barnes's here. To make these mountains a bit safer for everyone. You want to live in nature, not be victim to it.

"Now, there's a serious matter concerning the wolves. The wolves in our lab, which we'd been . . . researching, were able to escape. A couple of months ago, in fact," Haxler paused politely as the assembly room filled with astonished chatter and outrage.

One angry man in back leapt to his feet and yelled, "Didn't you say you were making it *safer* for the people up here? And now you've brought a bunch of experimental wolves into the mountains and let 'em loose? What are you going to do about that, you and your damn lot of scientists?"

"Calm down, sir," said Haxler gently, though from between his dark, sunken lids lightning flashed. "We have a plan, but it requires your cooperation. There's nothing especially wrong with these wolves, we mostly simply examined their behavior. But it does mean there are more wolves around the mountains. Since we want to err on the side of caution, we should eliminate the escaped wolves as soon as possible—better safe than sorry, that's our motto down at the lab. Its difficult for most people to tell the difference between a lab wolf and a wild wolf, though, so I suggest you shoot any wolves you see on sight. I know some of you are still on the fence, even after all the conclusive evidence, about shooting a wolf. But it is better to shoot one before it causes trouble, which they all do eventually. I would recommend that the town organize a wolf hunt through either side of the woods, and simply kill all the wolves you find. Bring them back to us, we'll let you know which ones are ours, and we'll let you know when they're all accounted for. Remember that wolves are nature's killers, and slaughter mercilessly without remorse. They'd butcher everything around them, until the world was a wasteland, if they were left to their own devices. Finish off the wolves, and we'll all have made the mountains, and the world, more secure for our children."

Haxler stepped hastily off the podium in his odd, unsettling gait, and Barnes walked beside him. "Why did you do that? All that propaganda? You skewed everything, until none of it was true any more," the vet said angrily.

"Spare me your lesson on honesty," Haxler muttered as applause surrounded them. "We were paid to get rid of the wolves, weren't we? We just accomplished in one speech what a hundred different serums and implants couldn't have."

❖

Glen stood facing the Barren Lands. Clouds of deep grey hung overhead, and he could hear the raven's call from above. All was not right; he could sense it. Yet when men where concerned, as he was certain they were, no matters were clear-cut. The Barren Lands were especially quiet, and he could not even hear the stirring of the voles and mice among the grasses. The old wolf had been hardened by the deaths of his children and his mate, and now he stood fearless and resolute. Already he could catch the scent of Salyr's 'cars' and hear the far-off bridge creaking under their weight. This happened every day as the loggers went to work, but Glen could tell their purpose was far more menacing this time.

Under the cover of the Cloud Tree's branches, Rapid's eyes opened wide and he rose from his sound sleep. "Something is very wrong," he said with conviction.

"How do you know?" asked Coast, automatically checking the pups. Crystal was nosing a flower while Sprint pranced about the roots of the enormous fir.

"Call it a . . . premonition," Rapid answered. He froze when he remembered that those were the words he had used before Tundra had been slain. The feelings were more intense now and seemed to envelop the whole pack. Yet he felt they were strongest to the south. He sniffed the air. It was Glen! Rapid began to panic inside. Did he have the ability to sense events before they happened…or did he perhaps make them happen?

Rapid darted through the field toward the hill Glen was perched upon. "What is it?" the old wolf asked, age emanating from his tone. Rapid looked into his father's face, realizing that it was weathered, tired. The oncc-glistening mane had turned into a blunt, grizzled tangle of hair. His eyes were dull and doleful. The old wolf breathed heavily, laboring to coax the air into his lungs. Rapid was struck by what he saw in this moment of clarity.

"I sense something, father," Rapid warned. "Please, go back now, with the others."

Glen was silent. "The winds are shifting. Soon, we won't be able to smell men if they come. Take the pack into the woods quickly. I will call you back if the feeling of danger passes."

Rapid ran back, telling Timber to take the others deep into the forest and wait there. Timber insisted on staying, but Rapid growled a warning that it was Glen's wish.

After the last of the tails disappeared into the darkness of the forest, Rapid looked up at the sky. "Aynsen, now would be a good time." Then he returned to Glen.

"I told you to leave," Glen said through open fangs. His eyes bore furiously into his son's.

Rapid's ears turned back. "I must meet the danger with you. You are my father, and there is no warrior I'd rather stand beside."

"Look," Glen said, seeming content with his son's response. A small white figure worked stealthily through the tree stumps. So stealthily, in fact, that as it was now downwind, the wolves had not noticed it until it was almost upon them. It was a large dog, charging straight at them.

Rapid slid into fighting stance, his lip curled back. A *teyen*, leading men into their midst? It appeared to be built like a sled dog. Through the mist of confusion and tension that surrounded Rapid, it seemed to him that the dog was familiar. Rapid snarled ferociously. Glen silenced him. "Has the wind, in its changing, blown away your senses as well? It is Salyr!"

The tan-spotted dog darted past them, running down to the mountain ashes and looking wildly about him. Both wolves followed. The young dog had never lost his calm in his months with them, but now he seemed frantic. "The men are coming in great droves! The entire town seems to have mobilized. They're working their way through every inch of the woods, some with horses, some with hunting dogs. They're hunting for wolves! We've got to flee! Where are the others?"

Rapid cast one last glance into the Barren Lands. He could not see or hear any men, but that didn't mean they weren't there. All three headed toward the Cloud Tree, hoping that they could trace the others' path and warn them before the hunt was upon them.

When they reached the den the three paused, making sure that the others had continued into the woods and that there were no stragglers. "How did you find out about this, Salyr?" Rapid said as he quickly scanned the fields.

"The tow—" Salyr started. A violent report rang down the hillside, and the dog stumbled, letting out a cry of alarm. Horses were galloping over the hill with such speed that the Copperleaf had no time to respond. The men upon them stopped and fired again and again, and the three canines tried to dodge as best they could.

"They were downwind," shouted Glen as they made their way to deeper forest, now taking a different tack than the others. "I knew that hill was too dangerous." He glanced up at the men, recognizing one. What he saw filled him with a dark sense of dread. He grabbed Salyr's ruff in his teeth and pulled the dog up from the ground. The dog's lop-ear had been shot, leaving only ragged tatters of flesh. "Run!" Glen barked. "Don't let them catch you!"

Rapid and Salyr rushed through the trees together. "The horses can't follow on rougher ground," Salyr said. "We've got to work our way up to the lake."

Glen was racing toward them, but his gait grew ever slower, until he stopped altogether and faced the approaching horses, his head high and resolute. He howled soulfully, but the sound was cut short as a bullet pierced his chest. The horses stirred up dust as they pulled up to either side of him, and as the *tanah* tried bravely to stand, he vanished under a veil of dust and noise.

Rapid, stunned into mute horror by the death of his father, tried to keep going, yet he felt he should have fallen by Glen's side. Salyr was barking at him to move, that the horses and men and dogs would run them down at any moment.

Then the hunting dogs arrived. A large husky slammed into Rapid, knocking him into the dirt. He gasped for air, biting in fear at the dog. It backed away and Rapid scrambled after Salyr. His dog friend was already ahead, leading some of the hunting dogs away, taunting them. Hopelessness filled Rapid's body. '*The moment we noticed something was amiss, we should have run into the forest, like Timber and the others. I should have dragged Glen along, pulled him by the tail if need be! How foolish could we have been?*'

A bullet whizzed by Rapid's head, splintering the bark of an aspen in front of him. The men's voices and the sound of hooves told him they were not twenty yards away. He quickened his pace, in keeping with his namesake, and overtook Salyr. The two began to lengthen the space between themselves and the hunting dogs.

"The Washbourne is not far," said Salyr. "We're almost by the banks now."

"Then we should try to split the dogs up from the men; without *teyen* they cannot track us nearly as fast," Rapid said.

Salyr could barely keep his friend in sight. He attempted to maintain the other dogs' attention by calling them all the forest names he could think of, relenting only when they came so close as to snap at him for his insolence.

The sound of the horses' hooves slowed and then stopped altogether as the wolves reached rougher ground; far-off whistles could be heard, and some of the dogs broke off the chase. Three still remained, all big, burly animals who, with wild training, could easily have slain the two fugitives. "I think we have enough time to deal with the stragglers," Rapid growled, backtracking to aid Salyr. The battle was long and fierce, but in the end they slew one of the assailants, and the other two retreated, whimpering in fear.

"Now we must hurry," said Rapid. "I can hear the river, but it seems angered. Let us see." The two proceeded at a quick trot to the Washbourne. The unusually warm weather was melting the mountain snow. The Washbourne's banks were quickly being washed away as the river expanded with fresh water. The surface of the river looked volatile, whitecaps appearing where enormous boulders jutted out.

Salyr regarded it grimly. "This is indeed ill news. The Washbourne is swollen, and rough waters yield for none. Yet fording it is the best way to hide our tracks."

The water raced downstream and still the two stood unmoving. "We must choose quickly," Rapid said frustratedly. "We need to find the others before they are killed at the hands of these men." The black wolf resolutely placed a paw into the torrent. "I shall cross."

Salyr's paw entered the water beside his. "We shall cross together, old friend."

They were only a foot into the water when the river's icy grip seized them and dragged them in. Rapid tried to turn about, to grasp the shore with his paws, but the current swept them along. Farther away, gunshots echoed, five in a row. Rapid whined in anguish before the flooding Washbourne swept him beneath the surface. He could neither see nor hear. He opened his mouth to speak to Salyr, but water swept in, choking him. His body was flung into a dizzying spin as he was swept downstream. He felt a rock cut across his leg. It was a long time before he tried to gasp for air, but he only took in more water. Opening his eyes, he expected to see the whirling rush of whitewater. There was nothing. Without any strength, he started to relax, his muscles slackening. Then he became just one more piece of debris amongst the turmoil of brown and blue.

The moment Salyr found himself pulled in, he had yelped and lunged toward the shore, but the current was too powerful and had driven him underwater. He allowed his body to be pushed along the stream, hoping for the current to carry him back to the surface.

This tactic worked, and he was above the water just long enough to see Rapid and hear his friend whine; then the surge drowned out any sound and carried him under again. He inhaled what felt like a sea-full of water before he had sense enough to stop breathing in. He was in a state of complete shock.

Without warning, a large rotted branch struck the dog full in the chest. He yelped and was about to try and dive around it when he realized it might offer his only chance of survival. Putting a paw around the bark, Salyr looked downstream for any sign of Rapid. '*What a day*,' he thought as he was carried past quiet, sparsely vegetated sandbars. Several beavers sitting atop their dams regarded him curiously with small eyes which blinked rapidly, and one slapped its tail uncertainly. Salyr smiled inwardly as he passed them by, sweeping down the river's course. This was one of those few moments when he yearned to be resting upon a hearth in a home, yet that was a life he had forsaken.

He rested his head against the branch, his eyes alert for the black fur of his friend. He drifted downstream, cherishing the momentary peace, yet he knew that the Copperleaf might all be dead by now.

Salyr finally drifted up on the bank, the branch catching between the dirt slope and a rock. He crawled out from under the branch, immediately putting his nose to the ground. Allowing himself no repose, he began smelling along the riverside for a trace of his friend.

Chapter Nine

The first gunshot rang out, and Timber, startled, dashed away from the others toward the sound. They were by Laibrook, the stream they had followed on their journey to the northwest to the bridge. The small brook had swollen with snowmelt as well and was now fast becoming a river.

"What are you doing, *Honovi*?" cried Coast.

"I must find Glen and Rapid," replied the big wolf stubbornly. "The men are shooting at them, and I've got to get them to safety. They are my packmates."

"We are, too," said Coast. "And the pups must not depend on Maya and me alone to hunt for them. I'm not sure if my leg will ever truly heal right. If we lose all three of you, we may well be doomed."

Timber bowed his head, torn between the two paths. He was a warrior, first and foremost, and had never lost a battle. He had faced grizzlies alone and emerged victorious, even slaying one. To stand by while his pack was slaughtered by an evil he could not comprehend was to him unthinkable. Yet he was loyal to his pack, and knew his responsibilities. If Glen perished, he would be the next in line, and his place as heir meant that he had duties to perform. The highest of those was to protect the next generation. He sat, frustrated, and looked down at Laibrook's rising waters. "The rivers and streams are rising for some great purpose," he observed. "The men have stirred Nature to anger, I suppose. We must rely upon Nature, then, to protect us from them. To protect Glen and Rapid."

A hound was baying in the distance, and the pups listened curiously. Both trotted down the rocky incline that they were hiding atop, but Coast seized them hurriedly and dragged them back. Sprint whined, wondering what the hound was saying. Its baying grew louder.

Coast's white fur rose slightly. "They're hunting us," she whispered warily. "Men are coming, too."

"A lot of noise they make, too," Timber snorted. "Sometimes I wonder how they grew so powerful in the first place, crashing about like an old moose."

"It's their magic, unless you've forgotten Tundra's tales," Coast said. "But this is no time for sitting about. Come, the ground just gets higher. Look at all those boulders up there, that waterfall. We should head up the side, it will be difficult for men to find footing. I'm just worried about the pups. We've already tired Crystal out, I'm afraid."

The wolves hastily scaled the steep rock face, their eyes blinking out the spray from Laibrook Falls. Maya, who maintained her cheerful demeanor even in these circumstances, panted contentedly.

"It's been such a warm day, at least the water's cool," she laughed.

Timber, at the head of the group as they walked ever upwards single-file, replied gruffly, "Wonderful. As soon as we get to the top of this, we've got to cross the lake to loose our scent, so I suppose you'll be cooler soon enough." The Copperleaf fell silent as they kept picking their way through the stones, deep in concentration.

The hound finally appeared out of the brush beneath them, looking up at the five wolves making their way up the rocky slope. His baying became frantic, and men's voices grew louder behind him. The hound began unsteadily to attempt to pursue them. It stumbled on some pebbles, then stared up at the wolves hatefully as Maya mocked him. "This is a job for a Bighorn, or at most a wolf. You may as well go home."

"Quiet, Maya!" Timber said sharply. "We're almost to the top. The faster we make it, the less chance there is of the humans spotting us."

And sure enough, as two men emerged from under the tree cover, looking up at the small waterfall, they saw the last black tail disappear from the peak. They started after the wolves, guns slung over their backs, shouting loudly to the hound.

When the wolves finally cleared the rock face, they were met with a breathtaking sight, for the lake had swelled to a vast size. Behind it were a tangle of mountain streams which forever fed its thirst. The lake's currents were volatile, and the wolves worried about the crossing, as there were two waterfalls, one each to Laibrook and Washbourne, over which they could be carried.

"What shall we do now?" Sprint asked, with a backward glance to the men climbing almost hungrily up the rocky slope. His small blue puppy eyes looked pleadingly into Coast's, and he whined fretfully.

Coast searched the lake. The tips of beaver dams were visible, and she realized what they must do. "Timber! We must swim in between the dams! The current will be less volatile there, and we can stand upon the branches for support!"

Timber looked at his sister skeptically. "What of the pups? Do you think they are strong enough for such an ordeal? The current is far stronger than I imagined."

Crystal had collapsed among the ferns, panting heavily, her eyes half-closed. Sprint was lying down as well, though his body lay poised to dart away if the men came over the edge of the incline.

"It is our only choice," Coast said desperately. "I have become their mother, and I cannot allow them to be shot by men or torn apart by their *teyen*."

Timber grunted in understanding. The pups tried to stay atop the beaver dams when they found one, but swimming between them was difficult for the two youngsters. Even the older wolves had to fight the current, and seemed to be drawn ever closer to the falls. When they were most of the way across the lake, they saw the men at the far bank bringing their guns to bear. Their shots went wild, for the wolves kept low in the water. Crystal, however, was standing on the beaver dam as they fired, and, startled by the noise, had fallen into the water at a particularly vicious part of the lake. Utterly exhausted, she hadn't the strength to fight the pull of the river, and as the others watched in horror she fell over Washbourne Falls with a frightened yelp.

Timber howled mournfully, but the men, thankfully terrible

shots, were unable to shoot him as he stood there defiantly. Then he stared at them, his golden eyes filled with malice, and they were struck with such fear that they nearly dropped their weapons. Before they could collect themselves, the Copperleaf had vanished into the far side of the woods.

"They're lost, they don't know where we are!" said Maya enthusiastically. The hunters were scanning the woods, but their questing eyes could not find the wolves amidst the hedges, from which they watched the humans warily.

"Don't be too confident, Maya," warned Coast. "We're not sure of that." Coast's body trembled for fear of Crystal. They had seen her swept over the edge of the falls, seen the little grey wolf disappear amidst the angry white water. Sprint was shaking uncontrollably, and Coast turned her attentions to him, so that they might both be comforted.

"The time has passed to worry about those two," Timber said as he watched the hunters dejectedly retreat down the rock face. "There may be others, however. I heard horses' hooves far off, and it sounded as if many dogs were loose amongst the trees. We must stay on our guard. Give these hunters a moment to depart, then we shall start searching for Crystal along the river."

Maya, ever curious, sniffed intently at a bush. "Come back, Maya," cried Timber in an exasperated tone. As the little black wolf nosed about the leaves, a covey of grouse took flight. A moment later, Maya returned with a dead bird, her eyes bright.

"Maya, we haven't time for that right now," Timber chided. "Our sister may have been killed. Our father and our brother are in danger."

"They'll need their strength when we find them, I suppose," Maya justified.

Timber snorted and ignored the yearling, turning his attention to the banks. As the afternoon waned, men's voices were still to be heard in the distance, but the small group continued their search. Sprint, straying from the other three, had run far downstream, exhausted though he was. He yipped excitedly and the others dashed to meet him.

"Crystal and Rapid are here," he said in elation. Both were on the opposite bank, but the water was shallower in this region, with a sandbar in the midst of it, and the wolves were able to cross due to the lull in the current.

Sprint had already crossed and was standing beside his sister, who lay limply in the mud. Rapid's body was several yards away, partly in the river, with the waters lapping gently around him. "I think they're . . . dead," Sprint said sadly. The others quickened their pace.

Timber gave a sniff to each body. "Don't be ridiculous. Glen needs to teach you some simple smells. There's no Death here. Honestly, you pups. . . ."

"Please, Timber. Now is not the time," Coast murmured from behind him, shaking herself off. "Rapid?" she whispered in her brother's ear. She licked his face. His body was cold, his fur soaked through. His leg was cut deeply. She gently cleaned the wound, then lay down by him and rested her head over his shoulder. His body quivered from the chill. "Why must we go through this?" Coast asked herself. "We have done nothing, yet we pay dearly for it. What ancient wrong have we committed that has warranted so great a slaughter?"

Timber looked upon his sister grimly. "We have done no wrong. There is simply no place for us amongst the humans. They wish to take the world for themselves—and make no mistake, they will. At the expense of everything else. What wrongs did the gentle forests commit, as they supped upon the cool winds and the fertile soils? None. Yet they were hewn down, and the animals which lived beneath them driven out. Thus were the Barren Lands created, the home of hundreds of creatures destroyed, so that the men, rather than live under the trees themselves, could live under their corpses. Salyr said once that they would not stop until the whole world becomes a Barren Land. I agree with him."

Maya also lay by Rapid, placing her paw on his tail. She did not heed the older wolves' talk. It was Rapid—her favorite brother, the one that cared for her and protected her in the lab—that mattered now, not men's grandiose plans for Nature's destruction. She remembered when she was the size of a hare, and how he used to bat his tail in front of her. She'd grab on gently with her teeth, wrestling with him, as he panted happily. She whined, softly taking the end of his tail in her mouth, then returning it to the mud. Would they ever play again?

She remembered her hunger as a pup, and how his silhouette at the entrance to the den always used to bring her comfort. She would rush to meet him, licking his muzzle anxiously until he would regurgitate some warm meat for her. She dropped the grouse beside his limp form. '*For all the food you've given me in times of need,*' she thought. Then she and Coast moved his body higher on the bank, for it was half-submerged.

Sprint was holding his own vigil by his sister's side. He licked her cheek and chin. He lay his chest across her flank to warm her cold body. The delicate little animal remained motionless, not even shivering as Rapid had.

Timber's ears perked up and his nose quivered. "Salyr!" he shouted, running down the bank. The spotted dog approached, his steps unsure, staggering through the mud and sand. His features were haggard, and his lop-ear, which had given him the appearance of a jester, was shredded. He was soaked as well. "Where is Glen?" Timber asked intently.

Salyr turned away, not speaking. His tail was bowed between his legs.

"Well?" asked Timber again, his throat seeming to grow thick so that he could not breathe.

"Look!" called Coast. By her side, Rapid coughed and spluttered, spewing out river water. His eyes opened slowly, returning Coast's intent gaze with a bleary-eyed stare.

His body jerked suddenly and he tried to get up. "Glen!" he cried. Finding he could not rise, he sank to the mud, his head low. "Glen is dead!" he whimpered at last in a weak voice.

A gasp escaped the pack. Salyr lowered his head, looking at the river, and whined. "We were ambushed. Glen was right, the hill was a blind spot. The men were downwind. They came on horses, and got a few shots off before we could even come to our senses."

"How did he die?" Timber asked.

Rapid raised his head and murmured, "They shot him. He slowed to face them, to fight them, to give us time to escape. Then the dust . . . it rose into the sky, and he was gone." The black wolf's eyes closed again.

All eyes returned to Salyr. "We took to the woods and aimed to lose our scent by crossing this river. We heard gunshots—they must have been firing at you. The current proved too strong and we were swept away. I held onto a branch and was carried almost as far as Dolsty Falls down by Lookout Point. That would have been my end if the branch hadn't stuck. Then I went looking for Rapid."

Coast spoke, nuzzling Rapid. "When the men fired, Crystal fell from the beaver dam. She was swept over Washbourne Falls, as I think you call it. Yet she does not seem to wake."

Timber was watching the unconscious pup nervously. "She has stopped breathing . . . What's to become of her?"

Rapid arose, then looked at the limp grey wolf. "She'll be all right." It was the same sense that he had felt earlier before the hunt, and when Tundra had died, yet this time it relayed a more hopeful message. There was something in his tone as he said this that comforted the rest of the pack. He walked up and gently pressed his paws upon Crystal's chest, then nudged her into changing position. A moment later she, too, coughed up water.

The pack hesitated, for she did not open her eyes. Everyone stood, speechless, unsure whether to rejoice or to mourn. Then a little whine escaped her lips. Her eyes fluttered open, and she whispered her littermate's name.

"The water . . . dragged me under, and I couldn't surface. I fell asleep. My head hurts horribly." The little wolf began to whimper.

"You will heal by tomorrow," assured Rapid. Her recovery puzzled him as he asked himself a question he had posed many times before. How did he know things before they happened?

"We have to move," Timber said. "Those hunters are still going to be combing the woods for us."

"I doubt that's an option," Rapid said. "Crystal's hurt, and we can't risk moving because of that bump on the head. Besides, I'm not in the best shape myself."

"You're right, of course," Timber conceded. "Then what are we to do?"

"There is a way that might work. I'll need you and Coast to get to work digging out a den here by the riverbank. Don't make it too conspicuous."

"They'll be searching for us here," said Timber warily.

"Yes, but they won't expect us to have built a den. What are the odds of them searching for us in one of dozens of small waterside holes? We're splitting up, anyway."

"Why?" asked Sprint.

"We don't wish undue attention, so we need the hole to be quite small. Just large enough for Crystal and me to crouch unseen within it."

"Perhaps we should build it on the sandbar," motioned Timber. "I doubt the men will look there."

Salyr spoke. "The river is still rising. We need the den as far up the bank as possible so it won't flood."

Timber and Coast dug hastily, for the haggard fugitives constantly heard the sounds of hooves, men's voices, and dogs in the distance. Occasionally the sounds would seem to grow quite close, and the pack would scatter, some even hiding between the ferns on the sandbar. In the late evening, as the sounds of men and *teyen* grew more and more infrequent, the wolves finished digging and scattering the fresh dirt to conceal the fact that the hole was freshly dug.

"Rapid," said Timber, regarding his brother with concern, for he still lay on his back, taking in deep breaths of air, "with Glen gone, we no longer have a leader. I know I was to be next, but now is not the right moment for me to head the pack. These times require someone with ingenuity and cunning, traits which are your strengths. I shall follow you now, for I bestow upon you the title of *tanah*." The two brothers stood by the rushing river, one a massive titan of a wolf, the other small and introspective, and there passed an understanding which formed between them an even closer brotherly bond. For Rapid would not rule as Glen had done, by leading the pack almost exclusively by his own expertise; instead, he would rely upon his siblings to guide for him, so that each of their strengths could be complemented by the others'.

"Thank you for the honor, Timber," Rapid said earnestly. "But time is of the utmost importance. Pick a place across the fields and wait for us there. As far as I know the men aren't hunting on that side of the woods. Perhaps they knew we were at the Cloud Tree." This thought seemed to occupy him, and he looked at the rushing river for a long while before he addressed the pack again. "Follow the river to Dolsty Falls, as Salyr calls it, then continue to Lookout Point. Wait by the tallest tree. Any concerns?"

Sprint stepped forward, his awkward paws wobbling after the stressful day. "I want to stay here, with Crystal," he said resolutely.

There was something in his manner that said he would not back down, and the older wolves smiled and thought of Glen at this.

"Very well, but you do as I tell you," Rapid said harshly. Sprint and Crystal ducked into the freshly dug hole, tucked between two river ferns. Without a sound, Maya, Coast, Timber, and Salyr crossed the sandbar in single file and disappeared into the distance. Rapid hoped they didn't face any trouble, for he could sense the fatigue in all their bodies: Salyr's slight tremble, Timber and Maya's slower pace, Coast's resurfaced limp. He couldn't help but wonder if there was something more to their exhaustion.

Rapid shivered, though whether from hypothermia or apprehension, he wasn't sure. He kneaded the soil beneath him with his toes, then settled down to rest.

Rapid drifted off and did not awake until later in the night, when a warm rain began pattering on the roof of the hole. At first he thought that it was the rain itself that had waked him, but there was an unsettling feeling in his stomach that told him otherwise. His ears strained to hear past the patter, and he heard a horse cry out in the distance. His eyes widened and he checked the pups, who were sleeping soundly.

The pups were his responsibility now, he realized, as was the rest of the pack. He was old enough to handle such a test of leadership, having seen six years on the Earth, but the magnitude of the task shocked him. How had his father cared for them all? Rapid and Coast had been ready to leave and start their own pack before the man Haxler had captured them. Afterward, they had decided that as soon as Paloke's pups were born, they would leave. Then Paloke had gotten sick and passed away, and the responsibilities of surrogate mother had fallen on Coast's shoulders. Now Rapid had been granted the obligation of being the *tanah*. That's what he had wanted in the first place, but he always wished to have his own whelps some day. To have the added responsibility of watching over the rest of his family as well was a bit overwhelming!

Maybe he was just not destined to start his own pack. After all, he had his family here. Perhaps later, after Rapid led them to safety, Timber could take over the Copperleaf, and Rapid could strike out on his own. Even then, there could be so many in a litter—some packs he had known had nine or ten cubs to watch over! Maybe it was all right to have his family here with the Copperleaf Pack. They could all share the responsibility of caring, teaching, and playing with the next generation, and all would be the better for it.

He realized that the pack *did* share the responsibility; it didn't fall on the *tanah* completely. The more members of a pack there were, the more the duty was shared. The help one gave to the other was always reciprocated in some way. No kindness ever went unrewarded . . . so it was with the circle of all living things . . . even humans, he supposed.

He snapped out of his reverie as the horses drew closer. He could hear the men as they slid off, and the click of a flashlight as it was turned on to scan the riverbank. The men were too close now. Rapid saw Crystal awake and Sprint crouched in terror. The pup darted toward the den mouth to escape, but Rapid was faster and caught him by the tail so hard that beads of blood began to collect on the hairs.

"Let me go!" whimpered Sprint. "They're coming again! They'll kill us!" He strained against Rapid, but the older wolf reeled him back into the den. Sprint bowed down and whined, turning to face the back of the den.

"Quiet! They haven't brought dogs, so they're not tracking us. I'm not sure what they're looking for, but we're a lot safer in here than we are out in the open. This hole is deep. They'd have to look pretty far in to find us. Sit here and wait."

Barnes ran along the bank, one hand brandishing a large flashlight. He brushed away the bead of sweat forming at his brow. Even at his prime as a man of twenty-two he was beginning to tire. His nerves throbbed. The river was rising, but it probably wouldn't overflow enough to pose a serious problem to the outlying cattle ranches. To the other three men accompanying Barnes, the river was their focus, for they had heard from the men who had traveled out this far during the wolf hunt that the Washbourne was rising, swollen with melting snow.

The object of Barnes's attention was quite different. The lab wolves had been spotted here; Haxler had shot the old alpha male himself. Barnes remembered that the old male's mate had been pregnant before the wolves escaped. Today a pup had been seen, presumably with the lab pack, that had been carried away as it tried to cross the rushing waters. Was it one of the alpha female's pups? How was the pack faring after all their tests? How had the CDLs influenced their lives in the wild? Barnes wished that they would run far away now, far from Dolsty, to escape Haxler. He knew that his partner would not relent in his hunt for the wolves now that he knew they were alive and thriving in the wilderness. Barnes felt a strong sense of guilt, but money was hard to gain up in these mountains, and if he ever wanted to escape this place he would have to have enough money to make his way in the outside world. The lure of 'civilized society' pulled strongly at the young vet, though he had only a taste of it during college. Apparently, he mused bitterly, that taste was tempting enough for him to risk his soul to get more.

What if the wolves were still here, hiding along the bank? It was a feeble hope. He simply wished to see that they were still in good health, still vibrant and alive, that their spirits had not yet been broken. Then he would leave them to live their lives as best they could.

He watched the gaps between the trees carefully for some glint, some phantom reflection of the flashlight in mysterious eyes. He stepped quickly, for the other men would turn back home soon and it would seem odd if he stayed alone. Suddenly, with a short gasp of surprise, he found his face in the mud: he had tripped over a tree root and lay directly in front of a little hollow in the bank. The flashlight had fallen nearby, and it lit the hollow, revealing two small pups and one of the black males from the lab. Barnes laughed as the three stared uncertainly at him, clearly frightened.

"What's going on, Jon?" asked one of the other men, walking up behind him. His tone of voice revealed that he thought it strange for someone to be lying face down in the mud, laughing uncontrollably.

Barnes quickly turned off the flashlight and rolled over. "Nothing, nothing. Just fell face-first in the mud, is all. Haven't done that since I was a kid."

The man nodded understandingly and gave him a hand to stand up. "Come on, then. The rest of us are heading back, going to catch some sleep. Doesn't look like the river's anywhere near floodin'."

Barnes walked with them, yet he silently resolved to turn his horse around at the earliest opportunity and try to get a closer look at the wolves.

As the horses' hooves grew distant, Rapid growled with unveiled animosity. "Barnes. I should have known. I smelled the man Haxler when they murdered Glen."

"Who's Barnes?" asked Sprint, blue eyes curious.

"He and another man named Haxler captured and tortured the Copperleaf Pack. It was a time before you were born."

Sprint took this in thoughtfully. He would be a fine packmate when he reached hunting age, for he planned out his actions and words. "How did you get away?"

"One of your late brothers, Tundra, found a way for us to escape, but . . . he never made it," Rapid related sadly.

"Was Maya alive?" asked Crystal.

"Yes, she was," laughed Rapid, some of the tension easing in his voice. "Full of as much pep as she has now, although half the size."

"Was mother unhurt?" asked Sprint. The torrent of questions from the two was usual for young wolves; there is much to learn about the world before you are left to it.

"Yes, and a lucky thing, too. She was pregnant with you at the time," answered Rapid. "We're going to have to leave now, if Crystal is ready for travel. I don't like the fact that Barnes spotted us."

"I'm ready," said Crystal, getting to her feet. Her knees buckled slightly. "But not too far," she added.

"Do we have to leave because Barnes saw us?" asked Sprint, already crouched at the entrance to the hole, peering up at the raindrops.

"Yes. I'm sure he's getting ready to capture us, now that he knows where we are. Rest assured he'll be back."

The three wolves trotted slowly down the bank into the misty darkness, following the others' path. Sure enough, not long after they had passed Dolsty Falls, Barnes came running, flashlight in hand, to the makeshift den. He wanted to see them, to discover how they were doing, to see that they were safe . . . perhaps to help them in some small way. But they were gone. How many wolves had survived the atrocities of the lab, he wondered sadly?

Chapter Ten

As soon as the rest of the pack caught sight of them, Rapid and the pups were ushered to safety under a tree canopy. The three were thankful to be away from the open fields, though the men had long ago returned home. Coast watched Crystal's unsteady gait with a mother's critical eyes. She was assuming Paloke's role more and more as time went on. "She can walk now," she said to Rapid. "That's good to know."

"Yes, but she's a little shaky on her feet," said Rapid. "We'd better get back to the rendezvous point."

As the group of survivors trotted toward the site they had picked to hide in, Salyr was deep in thought. The others curled up to sleep beneath the cover of a large boulder, but he sat in the rain, his tattered ear hanging down in front of his face, his muzzle etched with lines of concentration. He stared out through the spider web of branches to the grey clouds. Timber stayed with the dog, noting the wind and the muggy dampness in the air. "What worries you?" the wolf asked. There were certainly enough things to choose from.

"If perhaps I had run faster, I might have been able to warn you. I do not know if I can reconcile that."

"You told me when I mourned for Wrath that 'ifs' are for humans to live by. I would expect you least of all to fall into human ways." Timber spoke earnestly.

"That means much coming from you, Timber," Salyr said with a half-smile. "When I first joined you I wondered if you ever could see past the *teyen* in me."

Timber snorted dismissively. "There is no *teyen* in you, Salyr."

Salyr's manner was distant, still watching the clouds pass overhead. "Oh, there is, there is," he murmured. "Far more than I'd like. I fight it, but it's always there." The dog's blue eyes grew cold. His tone was bitter. "The men have taken Glen's life and his body from us. Why should I not take their 'ifs'?"

"Because they are worth nothing," Timber said. "Empty thoughts to drive you to sickness." The big wolf joined the others beneath the boulder.

'*It is tearing me apart*,' Salyr thought bitterly. '*This life—it seems to go against my grain. I wish to serve men, to lay by the fireside, to be fed at mealtime. Yet at the same time I despise them so, that I wish I could be finished with them forever. Why must these urges compete?*' He sighed aloud helplessly. '*More importantly, which will win?*'

⊠

Salyr's dreams had been plagued by the day's horrors, and he awoke trembling to find that all was quiet and the scent of men had disappeared. Yet his dreams had brought with them a revelation. He quickly nudged Rapid awake. "We must depart at once, old friend."

Rapid shook himself, then looked wildly about. "I don't sense any people. What is wrong?"

"Yesterday, on my way here, the woods were alive with gunfire on either side of me. Up by Greymane's especially. Haxler might have remembered where you fellows lived and ordered the hunt up there, as well."

Rapid was alarmed. Greymane had been a hated adversary, yet his malice was not unprovoked; the Copperleaf had done much in the past to antagonize his pack. Rapid had always feared that their escape from the lab would bring Haxler's evil work upon other wolves, and if their actions had caused Greymane's death. . . .

"Coast," he said, nuzzling her. "We must travel to Greymane's at once. The men . . . may have hunted them. Haxler might have even captured them."

Coast looked into her brother's eyes with horror. "Do not say such things; they must not come true."

"Whether they have or not, we shall soon see. It is quite out of our ability to save them," Salyr said. The others were left at the den, for it was to be a long journey and hostility was not expected on Greymane's part.

⊠

"Greymane?" asked Rapid warily. "Wayward? Any of you about?" The rain was heavy, followed by dull rolling thunder, and the three had difficulty trying to place the sounds they heard. It was rather like hearing many echoes, each equally loud, canceling each other out like static. The silence that followed was disconcerting, however. They were nearing the heart of the Frostwind's territory, and still no guardians had confronted them. It was late in the evening, though the clouds hid time from the wolves, and it seemed as if the dark grey skies were eternal.

Salyr trotted toward Rapid, jumping over a rock gully. "Look, Rapid, we've combed the area long enough. It's obvious they have deserted the place. And there's no telling when men might return. Their scent covers everything."

"Yes, but it's not fresh. It's not humans I'm worried about. There's a faint hint of something in the air . . . but the wind's hiding it. It makes me uneasy, but I don't think we're in danger."

"I can't agree with you on that one. You're the *tanah* now, though. All the same we'd better find Coast and leave this place. If the Frostwind do come back, they may not be too enthused to find us nosing about their grounds the moment they've gone. And last I checked, we'll be far outnumbered."

Coast barked shortly several times, and the other two joined her. She was sniffing intently at a track in the ground. It was near a large fir and the rain hadn't washed it away. The shape was unmistakable—a man's boot. Salyr wished the air were not so damp, so that he'd be able to smell who it was. He knew well enough, though. "Haxler was here, too," Coast said mournfully.

Rapid growled. "I'm beginning to trust Salyr's judgment. We'd better leave."

"Please, Rapid, they may still be around. There is no doubt now that we've brought this upon them. We must try to find some trace. . . . "

"It will do no good," Salyr said solemnly. "You know as well as I that the rains have washed away most scents. I doubt whether you could even smell blood on a log."

"There are other ways to find them than scent," Coast said. Then, she howled, her cry piercing the wind which carried it. All three hesitated, and a weak moan from the side of a distant hill answered back. Rapid and Coast looked cautiously at each other.

Salyr was skeptical. "That could have been the wind, or an echo. But let us check." He ran towards the sound and the others followed. "Look!" he cried. At the base of the hill was the Frostwind den. Several grey mounds lay around it, and the entrance was caved in.

Salyr sniffed. "Some of the new pups, and one of the mothers," he said sadly. "They've been shot . . . the one that called to us is not here."

Rapid was sniffing at the caved-in den. "I smell fire . . . ashes . . . They started a fire, then trapped some of the other wolves inside." The black wolf stumbled back in horror, the magnitude of Haxler's hatred striking him suddenly.

"They've done it. They've declared war on wolves," Salyr whispered resignedly.

"War?" asked Coast. The wolves stared blankly, for they did not comprehend the word.

"The humans will rise up, with their guns and traps and poisons, and they shall not stop the killings until every last wolf is dead. Their bloodlust stems from their hatred: it is unwarranted, but it is there. That hatred is why I left people. It is almost on a whim that they find something to hate; for it is not the object of their hatred that matters, merely that they hate it. Most often their anger is directed at one another, but it appears that Haxler, or someone equally powerful, has directed it against the wolves. It will rage like the storm, and will only be satisfied when nothing is left."

The wolves shook in horror at Salyr's portent. There was evidence of the war—until now a foreign concept to them—all around them, in the smell of ashes, of blood, of Haxler, in the little bodies that lay on the wet earth below them, and the other wolves' corpses which they began to perceive during flashes of lightning upon the slopes and in the ditches.

The low moan, its strength departing, called again from the top of the large hill. The trio sped up to its source beneath a fir tree. It was the massive Greymane, the glint dimming in his golden eyes. As he realized the newcomers were from the Copperleaf, he lay his head down resentfully. "I suppose you'll slay me now. It would be the kindest act." The ground stank of blood, and as the wolves looked they found the big *tanah* had been pierced by three bullets.

"If that is your wish, old rival," Rapid said kindly. He understood the agony Greymane must have endured, and awaited the command.

"They . . . came without warning. As if they knew we were here. All around us, my packmates fell as our ears were filled with deafening noise. Then they lit the den. Kaya and her litter couldn't get out. Teril's did, but the men struck them with their sticks. The pups fell dead amid the loud cracking noises. My attendants and I tried to push the other wolves up the hill, but more were struck down before they could begin. We'd had a big hunt, and we were all meat-drunk; no one was quick enough. Even in our best shape we wouldn't have made it. The men had horses—those trampled some of my youngsters. . . . Wayward was struck down behind me." The wolf's eyes were glazing over. "I don't understand . . . why. . . ."

The rain subsided as Greymane died. The three Copperleaf remained amidst the destruction. Coast questioned herself in vain, trying to discover a reason for such cruelty. Rapid, however, simply looked at the old male lying limply under the fir. Salyr watched with concern. The philosopher within Rapid, who had spent the long nights of his life gazing out into the sky and thinking of the wonders of the world, seemed to melt away. Rapid's demeanor grew icy and Salyr could see his muscles grow taut with tension and resolve. "Haxler came here because he was looking for us. When he realized this wasn't our pack he let the other men slaughter them. At times in the pen I sought solace in the fact that his cruelty didn't extend to other packs. No bodies adorned the walls. We alone suffered, and the knowledge that somewhere beyond the fence other wolves roamed free gave me comfort. Now, he's drawn innocent wolves into it!" Rapid snarled. "Every wolf in the mountains will die because of us! I must save them—Haxler's madness must end!"

The black wolf stormed back to the rendezvous point in a trance, running and stumbling through the woods at an incredible speed until he fell to the ground, exhausted. His head felt light and as he looked up into the trees he saw them spinning about in circles. He could not yet understand the sickness these sensations foretold, nor the reason for it, but when Salyr found his friend collapsed in a daze, he felt a grim fear grip him.

No stars were visible between the treetops, but all pretense of rain had stopped. Rapid had recovered from his spell before returning to the rest of the Copperleaf, and after sleeping part of the night through he decided it was time to address them. The night was pitch black, but the wolves could sense each other's warm bodies and their rich individual scents.

"Timber, the one we all anticipated would someday rule the Copperleaf, has transferred the title to me for the time being. I am very grateful for it, and shall rule until he sees fit to take over. I have chosen Coast as the *maisa*, if she will accept."

Coast's ears rose and immediately she struck a more regal pose, her tail held high. "I shall accept readily, Rapid. Thank you."

"I will not be as strict as Glen. There are some transgressions I will allow that he did not; for instance, as long as there is enough food at a kill site I believe we should have equal turns at it." Timber growled angrily, muttering that this sort of thing was 'just not done.' "I know it is not the right way," Rapid continued. "But we wish to survive as a pack, and I believe it is the best way to do so. Now, I won't let the pack go to the *Nesnya*, so you shall still show due respect for the hierarchy. The only reason the weaker shall eat with the stronger if there is ample food is that we must *all* stay alive if we are to survive. Tundra, Paloke, Wrath, Glen—all lost in the past several months. We cannot afford another death. All of us have attributes vital to keeping the pack together; remove one of us and the others may not survive the humans' war." Rapid explained what a war was to those who had not journeyed to the Frostwind's territory. "As you may have heard, it seems we were quite fortunate that only Glen perished in the hunt yesterday. Greymane's entire pack—from the pups to Greymane himself—all were murdered by the humans. I shall not elaborate for sake of our own pups. Haxler, however, is the man that killed them—" everyone gasped at this. Timber growled, his lip curling into a snarl. "—No doubt as he was looking for us. It seems as if he is leading the humans' cruel actions toward us."

He hesitated briefly. The other wolves were terrified by the news he had brought. "The man Haxler cannot be stopped. He is scouring the woods for us. If we stay here he will find us and run us down. We will suffer the same fate as Greymane's pack, or worse yet, be taken back to the lab. I lead the Copperleaf now, and I cannot allow that to happen. That is why I say we must move again. I propose we go far past Washbourne Lake, close to the mountains. We will leave at dusk two days from now. I want Timber and Maya to do a little scouting; you should probably leave now. If you wish to hunt something to keep your bellies full, I recommend it. As many of us as possible should travel well-fed. Salyr, as for you, I'd like you to return to town. Look around and tell me what you find. I want to know what Haxler is planning. But be careful. The men shot at you, and may know you by sight now."

Rapid was waiting by Lookout Point. The sun would sink below the mountains but a little more before they would depart. The *tanah*'s long black hair ruffled in the breeze. None of the scouts had yet returned. Long into the night Rapid had reviewed the past few days in his mind, remembering the condition of his packmates, and had come to a conclusion. He could only tell Timber about it, for he knew only the great warrior would understand. He would wait until the pack journeyed to safer ground. The others had met his orders with questioning glances. Why still stay anywhere near the town? They could move far, far away and never be near humans again!

Rapid thought about his father, who had died after ten years on the earth. What a blow his death must have been to the pups! Their mother and father had died before they were barely old enough to comprehend the Death scent! Rapid realized that his own childhood had been a happy one. He used to play long hours with Timber, Wrath, and Tundra. Cuddling up to his brothers in the den when at night the haunting call of an owl came from outside in the great Unknown, climbing over their bodies to arrive at a teat first when he was hungry: those were his memories. That was before more men came. Long before the Barren Lands even started, when the East and West Dolsty Woods were joined together.

In comparison, these pups were spending their childhood in a living hell. No more than bundles of fur, they nursed from a mother whose weak milk never gave them a full stomach, merely sustained them. Instead of the soft, gentle breathing of a mother in her prime, they heard the labored breath of a distressed animal. Instead of two parents to cuddle them and play alongside them, they had a tired mother and a stressed father, both holding to life with the hope merely of seeing their children free of the lab's tortures. When they were no more than rambunctious pups budding with wolfhood, their mother died, and their father was brutally murdered by the humans who, in Rapid's days, were not a threat.

Only a few months ago, all his littermates were together.

Unhappy, tortured, but together. Now he had Timber, but. . . . The loss of Wrath and particularly Tundra left a void in his life that could not be filled. The poet and the philosopher, he thought ruefully. The poet was dead now, and the philosopher . . . the philosopher hadn't died yet, just . . . hardened. These thoughts were not the ones which he had mulled over when he used to watch the quiet fields; his musings had grown more cynical, more morbid. He concluded sadly that his own peace of mind was yet another casualty of the laboratory experiments.

"Rapid!" Coast called, her white fur blowing in the wind. "You haven't slept at all?" she asked scoldingly.

"No," he responded in a bemused manner, not taking his eyes off the setting sun. "Although I must admit it sounds like a wonderfully refreshing idea. I'm not able to rest well lately. I'm not sure why, but the thoughts just keep on coming, or I watch the forest for something that isn't there. It's quite odd."

"I've been having trouble sleeping, too," Coast confessed. "Not because of any *specific* thoughts, really. More like their echoes. I'm not sure what to make of it. But I'm always able to fall asleep eventually."

"Count yourself the lucky one, I suppose," her brother said. "Look at the sun. Doesn't it appear to be falling, about to crash into the mountains? I wonder why it doesn't."

Coast watched her brother, still not taking his eyes off of the sun, and backed away slowly. That sounded almost like something the dogs at the lab would have said.

Rapid finally seemed to release himself from his strange musings. "How does it feel, being the only one left of your litter?"

"It feels . . . extremely lonely. I was in the womb with those wolves, and to think that I'm the only one left, that all of them are dead . . . well, it's a bit disheartening, to say the least."

Rapid was listening intently. "I was just wondering what it would be like to be the last one. I've lost Tundra and Wrath, and if I lose Timber, I don't know what I'll do."

"I'm touched," barked Timber's voice from across the field. He had a mischievous glint in his eye that meant he would mock Rapid for his sentimentalism later.

"What did you find?"

"There's a cave," Maya said anxiously. "Several miles past the beaver dams."

Timber elaborated. "It is reasonably close to the Washbourne. The cave itself is on a hill, but once you enter, it slopes down. It is sizable, much more than is needed for the few of us."

"Is the mouth of the cave large?" asked Rapid with concern. "We don't want too conspicuous an entrance."

"Yes, unfortunately," answered Timber. "It's about four wolves tail-to-tail across, about one-and-a-half high. However, it is tucked behind a lot of trees and inside a large rock formation. It looks more like the residence of a bear or mountain lion than a wolf pack."

"Is there a back exit?" asked Coast.

"Just large enough for me to scrape through," Timber said.

Rapid recalled 'scraping' under the fence at the lab. He growled as he remembered Haxler.

"What's wrong?" asked Coast in alarm.

"Nothing," Rapid assured her in an extremely evasive tone of voice. "I'm just going to catch some more shut-eye until Salyr gets back." The others agreed, and soon all were asleep . . . except Rapid.

Salyr blinked rapidly, for his eyelids seemed to want to stick together. He was quite groggy, and as he looked about sleepily he could tell he was in a cage. Other dogs barked all around him, senseless spluttering that he could not understand. Whether this was because he was drugged or because their noises didn't make sense in the first place, he couldn't altogether discern.

It was a long while before he was able to rouse himself enough to try to recall what had happened. He had been wandering about town, thinking that Rapid would be pleased; for though everyone seemed very energetic, 'wolves' weren't mentioned much, and it didn't seem as if another hunt would take place, at least for the time being. The people were gratified that so many wolves had been killed: seventeen had been slain that day. Salyr was leaving town by way of the road the wolves had crossed weeks earlier when a car pulled up behind him. Salyr had simply moved to the side to let it pass, but it did not. A man stepped out and tried to coax him into the vehicle, and when Salyr showed he would have none of it the man grabbed a gun and shot him. It was a tranquilizer gun, though Salyr didn't know it. The man was Barnes, hoping to replace the dogs that had died over the previous week.

Now Salyr was in a cage, in the very lab from which his wolf friends had escaped. What they would do to him he did not know, but judging by what the few surviving occupants of the cages around him were saying, it would be better to live in ignorance for a time.

He slept most of the day away and waited, unable to comprehend what the humans might be planning.

"We can't wait much longer if we are to arrive there before morning, Rapid," Timber said.

Rapid paced back and forth fretfully. "I can't understand it. What could have held him up? There must be great danger brewing."

"All the more reason to get the pups to safety," pressed Coast. Her green eyes were filled with worry. "For the men to have caught or killed Salyr does not bode well for us."

"Indeed it doesn't," agreed Rapid. "Very well. We've got to head out. He'll have to follow our trail, if he's still coming back."

Maya picked up an old elk bone, then growled through the corners of her mouth, "I'm ready to go!"

Rapid laughed, his mood lightening. He could always rely upon Maya to lift his spirits. "Maya, you silly pup!"

"Wolf!" she corrected, "Full-grown wolf!"

"Well, you wouldn't know it to look at you. Nor listen to you, for that matter. Come on, now, you cannot bring an elk bone. It's a long way to the cave, you said so yourself."

"It's still too close to the town," commented Sprint warily. "Are we going to live there long?"

"I hope not. You're growing wise, Sprint. Very good. I don't want a repeat of the wolf hunt as long as I live."

"Especially since you're the *tanah* now," laughed Timber. Rapid conceded the point.

"Are you ready to travel, Crystal?"

"I guess so," the blue-eyed pup said uncertainly. "My head hurts, but for the most part I'm all right."

"We're going to be traveling a long while, and you might get tired. If you do, we can stop." he assured her. Then he turned uneasily to his more observant brother. "Timber, the weather is such that it will be safe to stop, right?"

Stormy skies would not hurt the wolves; there was no way for the rain or sleet to penetrate their undercoats, but it was not ideal weather in which to travel. They could still move quickly, and their canine hearing would not be greatly obstructed by the pitter-patter of the raindrops, but the pack's vision would be impaired, and worst of all, the changing wind would be frustrating to catch a scent on. Wolves use the sense of smell as a radar, and without it on a night like this, they would be sensor-blind. If they caught a scent, they would be unable to discern from where it came. This was a great disadvantage, and one that could prove extremely dangerous.

Timber sniffed the air. "Not really. You know it's going to be bad, don't you? You just don't want to believe it. We're in for a horrible storm. In fact. . . ." The big wolf paused and rain began to fall. The downpour was so abrupt that it made Sprint start in alarm. The wolves began to move out toward yet another home.

"'Strange weather brings strange times,'" quoted Rapid from an old lupine adage. "And the weather we've been having is *quite* strange. Only a few days ago, the mountain snows were melting, and now this? I sense nothing but ill omen."

Chapter Eleven

'*Of all the nights to have a summer storm,*' Rapid thought, '*the Nesnya had to pick this one.*' Wind howled through the firs, and dark clouds sped through the sky above. The showers drenched the tired pups, and they blinked their blue eyes constantly in an effort to see the forest path ahead. Rapid howled back to the others. "Come on! Stay close together, lest we become separated. Make for the scent of the squirrel, if you can smell it: Timber left it as a marker." But the fickle winds had changed direction yet again, and the wolves could not rely on the scent to show the way.

Coast walked behind the pups, lifting their exhausted bodies by the nape of the neck or nudging them along, but she was worried that they would not last much longer. "It's several miles to the cave, Rapid. Are you sure we can't stop here for tonight?"

Maya piped in too, full of discontent and still talking out of the sides of her mouth, because she had refused to abandon her bone. "Why can't we stop? I'm tired and my jaws are getting sore."

"Maya!" Timber barked. "Rapid warned you that would happen, and now you're paying for it." Timber had spread out to the left flank, away from the others, to check for dangers. His senses were the sharpest of the Copperleaf, and it was safe, and indeed essential, for him to scout ahead occasionally.

"She may do whatever she wishes. If she wakes up tomorrow with a sore jaw, so be it. It'll be a lesson," said Rapid.

"I don't want to learn a lesson!" said Maya very loudly. The rest of the pack ignored her and she soon hung her head in silence. Yet she still gripped the bone stubbornly.

Timber was sniffing in all directions and fell back to join the others. "Rapid, are you sure we can't rest the night here? We're becoming disoriented, and I'm not sure that I can scout ahead any more. There's a much greater chance of us running into danger now, if anything wishes to bear this storm."

"No, we must keep going. Everyone, let's howl!" Rapid began to howl in a desperate bid to increase morale. He hoped it would lift their spirits enough to continue through the last stretch. A split second later Coast picked up a note, and within a minute the whole pack was howling in unison.

Rapid wondered where Salyr was. They had abandoned him, and he knew they were leaving, although he didn't know where they were going. '*As long as he doesn't get in over his head,*' Rapid thought. Rapid's own head was plagued by worries. The wind's direction was constantly changing, so it was nearly impossible to pick up any scent, including a human's. The pack, especially himself, should not have tired this easily, and all seemed as though a sickly pall had been cast over them.

'Aynsen will save us,' Rapid prayed. *'Aynsen will save us. . . .'*

Salyr awoke to a loud, wracking cough. One of the dogs in the next kennel, he assumed. There were three crammed inside a space no bigger than the span of his own body. Salyr stared at the hunched figures for a time. The coughing mutt met his gaze with beady, listless eyes. It was dark out, and the man—Barnes, he guessed—had left for the night. Salyr noticed that the other dogs in the lab had awakened at the cough as well, and they began to stir about fiercely. He could hear, as they began to bark and yelp, that many were quite mad, and he shuddered to think of the experiments that had been performed upon them.

He tried to curl up and fall asleep again, but he was disturbed by the Labrador above him banging on the top of his cage. "You're new here, aren't you? I should think you are. . . I . . . I haven't seen you before, and I see everything, you see. Ah, so you see as well! Wonderful, I wasn't aware. There aren't many like us, you know. You know too! Well, we must be kindred spirits, as my master used to say. Before he gave me to the men that live here. They're our masters now, so we'd do best to obey them."

Salyr, still curled up, opened one eye and said sulkily, "I don't have a master. Nor will I. If they intend otherwise they'll have my teeth to differ with."

"A spunky one! They never like that. You'd do best to sleep the day away, like I do. They've taken me out on that table only once, and the less you lay on it the better off you are. It's why I've lasted as long as I have. Now, take a look at that fellow that just coughed. Cougher, I've named him, on account of a recent stroke of genius I've had in the art of naming. Always barking he was, even when they drugged him. Cause a row like that and you won't last long; he's been here barely a week and he'll be gone before another passes."

"Oh, very nice, you heartless sod," cried Cougher indignantly. "How 'bout a bit of sensitivity for the dying?"

"Why should you receive such special treatment? We're all dying here; just some of us quicker than others. Say, what's your name, then?" he asked, turning inquisitively to Salyr.

"Salyr. I'd love to talk, but I'm going to take your advice and go to sleep so they won't pick me."

"I suppose it's a good thing to practice, but they're not about now: that's why everyone's barking. So you needn't sleep."

"I wish to, and so I shall," Salyr said gruffly. "And besides," he added slyly, "they watch you all the time, even when they aren't here."

The Labrador was quite stricken by this new information, and looked about frantically. He put his paws up to the top of his cage and whined hysterically. "Oh dear, oh dear. It's a wonder they haven't done away with me yet, with all the ruckus I cause when they leave. How can you see that they watch you? Oh, I forgot, you see everything too. Oh dear . . . I suppose I'd best go to sleep, too."

Salyr knew that there must be an escape route somewhere. The wolves had taken months to figure out how to escape their pen, and their freedom had been brought about by human negligence. Salyr would wait, then, and watch, anticipating a time when the men would give away some means of escape. Then Salyr would be off, leaving these haggard captives and returning to the woods and the Copperleaf.

❖

The cave was getting closer. "What a night to move, Rapid," cried Timber as the storm raged overhead.

Rapid leapt deftly over a rock, then glanced over his shoulder at his littermate. "Oh, hush. We were through this once already." The wind howled in their ears, obscuring any other sound. Crystal stumbled in her tracks, half-conscious from exhaustion, and Timber pulled her to her feet, his great jaws clamping onto her ruff. Rapid looked on with concern. "I can't see!" cried Sprint, his eyes squinting. Coast nudged him forward, and he continued blindly, a nervous whine escaping his lips.

"Yes, that's why we have to get to that cave," said Rapid, his voice full of frustration. He pushed forward in fury.

"This is pure madness!" cried Timber. He stopped and settled by the roots of a black hawthorn, his big tail protecting his face. A pink scar was still evident across it. He closed his eyes to sleep, and the other wolves followed suit.

Rapid became angry, growling threateningly. "Push yourselves!" Didn't I let us eat and rest for a day? I told you our goal, but you have quit. The Copperleaf do not surrender to the weather!"

Maya spoke out from under her tail, "We did not know the storm would be this bad."

The *tanah* rose to his full height, standing against the winds, sleet buffeting him from all sides. "Glen would be ashamed of all of you. You aren't acting like true wolves! What happened to your spirit, your energy? In times past a storm like this was a moment for happiness. We rejoiced in it and let the winds bathe us."

Coast, who had attempted to continue but stumbled to the ground, her limp too serious to continue, answered, "I can't understand why, but I feel tired, sick."

"So do I," added Maya and Timber. The pups remained silent.

Rapid thought for a moment, nose twitching in contemplation. "In a way, so do I," he admitted. "Still, that's not an excuse. We must press on."

The Copperleaf followed Rapid solemnly, a stumbling, ragged band of exhausted wolves. They trusted with blind faith that the *tanah* would fix what was wrong. They could feel the weight of responsibility on him, and could sense that he was being crushed beneath it. Rapid *would* fix things tonight, he *would* make it all better. There was a way. He knew now what he had to do.

Coast's body lay still, her white fur slowly rising with each calm breath. Her leg was held out from beneath her, gingerly lain at the bottom of the cave as if it pained her deeply. Rapid waited for her breaths to slow as he watched from the mouth of the cave. "It was a long journey. They showed great strength in accomplishing it, after all we've gone through," he said to Timber. He paused. "I posted us both as sentries so that I could talk to you in private."

"I thought as much," Timber said, sensing that something was dreadfully wrong. "Go on, Rapid."

The sleek wolf took a big breath, then let it out in a deep sigh. He turned to his brother. "I have a matter to which I must attend immediately."

"In this weather? What is it?"

"It is Haxler and the lab. I cannot let them slip from my mind."

"If he was down by the Lookout Point, surely he cannot find us now. He is no longer a threat We are safe here while we recuperate; later in the summer we can head northwest to be free of men forever."

"I disagree with you on several counts, Timber. The men will scour the hills all the way to the base of the mountains for us eventually. This isn't terribly far from Washbourne Lake, and the men easily pursued you that far. What is to stop them from coming up here?"

"They wouldn't . . . Not just for us. . . ." Timber whined.

"They would, and they did. We've lost Glen to them already; next time we may lose more. And Haxler is always at the forefront; I think he is the one who struck down our father. What did he do with the body? For I returned to the site and it had disappeared; all that was left was the scent of men, with Haxler's most prominent. Glen's Death scent trailed the ground with Haxler's into the Barren Lands. I fear the tests may not be over for us, not even in death." Rapid said this with such venom that the other wolves' ears flicked, sensing sound, though they remained asleep. Rapid and Timber waited in silence, listening to the rain patter on the roof of the cave and the wind whistle outside. "Haxler is alive and taking our bodies. He left the Frostwind's because they were of no worth to him. They want us . . . to test something . . . to see the results of something that they had done before. . . ."

Timber looked with concern at his brother. These conclusions were quite confusing to him, and he could not properly follow their logic. "Are you feeling all right, Rapid?"

"The question is, 'Are you feeling all right, Timber?' You said 'while we recuperate'. Coast's leg may need several days' rest before we continue, and the pups are tired, but what real excuse do you, Maya, and I have? Yet we act as if we are wounded, and feel as if we must recover from some sickness. We don't traverse vast distances the way we used to, and even Maya is not up to her usual pranks and high spirits. We have not been hurt in battle, nor have we eaten poisoned meat: we know the smell well enough, and would be long dead by now. The scent of *this* illness bothers me, for it is quite elusive. You can barely catch a whisper of it; yet it remains, and grows stronger. Thankfully, the pups do not have it: their exhaustion is merely the strain which our lives on the run are putting them through. This, combined with instinct, tells me that the source of our sickness is the lab. They've done something to us. Have you noticed how we always nudge those scars on our tails? They're always throbbing dully, and we're never free of the sensation. The pups, since they weren't born yet, weren't subjected to this experiment. I need to find out how we can get better again."

"You never would have been able to conclude all this, Rapid. What has happened to you?" Timber asked, his features gaunt with stress.

"I do not know, *Honovi*," Rapid said sorrowfully. "What has happened, indeed? Can we remedy it, when it has plagued us, unheeded, for so long? I shall not watch as we crawl away one by one to die alone, leaving the pups to fend for themselves in this dangerous world. I must leave quickly."

"What do you propose to do?" Timber looked up wonderingly at his brother, fearing an answer.

"I shall visit the Dark Place, the lab. I will have my vengeance, my lost kin's vengeance. Then I will see about this…thing."

"Where do I fit in? How do I help you…*to die?*" Timber's last two words were choked, and a whine escaped him. Maya stirred in her sleep.

"You will watch over the pack and see that they do not follow. If any wake, say I went out to hunt." At the end of Rapid's words Timber whimpered and rose, pacing anxiously back and forth. Both knew what would happen; both knew Rapid was going to his death. Rapid leapt to the threshold of the cave. "Do not forget me, my brother." With that he darted out into the darkness of the storm and disappeared. Timber walked down to the end of the cave where the others slept.

He glanced back toward the opening of the cave. "You are brave, my brother," he whispered. He curled next to Crystal and tried to sleep.

The rain splashed upon the ground. Rapid raced through the woods, adrenaline coursing through his body, faster than any would have thought possible of such an animal. He sniffed the air for a trace of Glen's Death scent. It would barely be present, mixed with a thousand other smells, but he hoped it would not have vanished in the storm. Timber would have been far better at finding such a faint whisper of their father's presence. Rain trickled through the trees and the forest echoed with the sound of thunder. The black wolf followed the Laibrook to where he hoped he could pick up his father's scent. Rapid's animosity grew stronger as he thought of the terrors of the lab, the hardships the man Haxler had put them through, and he pushed himself even harder. His breath began to rasp in wheezes and gasps, and foam began to form at his mouth. Finally, exhausted after hours of running, he spasmed and tumbled down beside a stump. In only a third of a day he had made it deep into the Barren Lands, a far greater distance than should have ever been possible. His body, weakened by the lab's sickness, shook violently, and he lay still.

Striving to overcome the powerful urge to sleep, to lay beside the stump and never rise again, Rapid stumbled a few feet only to collapse into a ditch. He vomited and fell unmoving. The hours passed until it was late in the day, and still he lay there, his eyes blinking vacantly, as if he were dead. The wolf was half-buried in mud, and, as the ditch filled with water, dirt and grime began to run into his mouth and eyes.

After a long time the wolf roused himself, barely aware, and stirred from the ditch, covered in mud. His five senses were mangled; yet he could rely upon his instinct to carry him through this time of need. It flowed through him, forcing his body into a state of half-consciousness. His body was numb, yet he could still feel. His eyes were blurred with filth, yet he could still see. His nose was perplexed in his sickness, yet he could still smell. His ears, though he did not know it, stirred to catch the sounds of the clearing, and his tongue lapped at the rain feverishly. Then he felt himself being dragged off the rocks over which he had fallen, for though he was not aware, his feet were bearing him, one slow, trembling step at a time, until he reached the top of the ditch. His eyes let the cleansing rain water run into them, and gradually his mind returned. He thanked the Earth and the *Aynsen* and was on his way to save the Copperleaf.

Glen's scent had all but faded away, but Haxler's was so distinct that Rapid was able to follow it at a fairly quick trot. Still, he was cautious of traveling too fast for fear of another seizure. If he was delayed like that again, there would be no hope of tracking the scent. As he raced across the bridge he became lost in sadness, thinking of his family. He would probably never see the loving Coast, courageous Timber, or playful Maya ever again, and if he failed to find out what was wrong with them, the pups would soon have no one to care for them. He knew it was a fool's quest he was on, but he could not give up hope. Rapid had a sense that somehow he would discover what was so very wrong and how to rectify it. It was still raining, though dusk was falling quickly; he had been away from the cave only a day.

Rapid was startled as he neared the old road, for he could smell very distinctly the scent of Salyr's blood. His lip curled to reveal his teeth and he let forth a low growl; the stink of the lab's chemicals, the ones that brought sleep, were unmistakable on the dirt beside him. He quickened his pace toward the lab. He hadn't an inkling what he would do once he reached there. Each step closer to it became more difficult to take, though he wasn't sure whether it was fear or the sickness that was laboring his progress.

Chapter Twelve

"The old male's body has been on ice for a while now, Barnes," Haxler said, eyeing him. "We need to find out what those CDLs have been up to since our pack escaped." He walked around the lab with halting, unsteady steps, taking notes on each of the dogs. Salyr lay in the corner of his kennel, his eyes watching the two scientists intently, but they took no notice of him: he was not needed yet.

"I'm almost afraid to look," Barnes said. Haxler let out a small laugh of scorn. "Those implants will deteriorate soon; the prototypes weren't meant to stay in this long. They'll eventually become infected, and who knows what other side effects might follow." He was concerned for the wolves and feared what the CDLs would do to them. They had not been installed with the greatest of care.

Haxler misinterpreted his worries. "The problem with you, Jon, is that you're a hypocrite. Your voice shows you fear those wolves just as much as those ranchers back in town. The only difference is that you hide it behind some kind of righteous animal-loving façade.

Just because you're a damn vet a couple of days a week doesn't mean you have to pretend feelings for every stupid animal on the planet. None of them are worth the effort. Look at those folks back in Dolsty: half of 'em that want the wolves dead own dogs themselves. Double standards are what we live by, they're human nature. Might as well get used to them."

Barnes sighed deeply. "I suppose I'll take a look at him now." He brought the limp grey body out of the cooler, its glazed eyes staring up at him, striking him with guilt. The old male wasn't in especially good condition; he had two bullets in him and had been beaten as well.

He drew a blood sample and analyzed it. When he had finished he bit his lip thoughtfully. There were signs of deterioration from the effects of the implant they had placed in the alpha wolf. Barnes could tell what had happened.

The implants' original purpose was to release chemicals to suppress the wolves' natural instincts, and to cause a type of non-aggressive depression which would make the animals more passive. There was a problem with this shipment of the devices, though. It must have been contaminated with a virus. Some foreign matter was eroding from the implant and infecting the bloodstream with whatever it carried. Slowly, red blood count decreased. As the CDL had eroded itself down to the core, the amount of foreign matter in the bloodstream would be considerable. Now that the infection was widespread, it had removed itself from the implant fragments and begun a takeover of the body. The effects seemed to accelerate exponentially. He compared the trivial amount of dormant virus which he was now able to detect in an old sample of Tundra's blood to the active virus running its course through the dead alpha male. The wolves were probably conscious of the virus's effects now. Barnes worked out some calculations on a scrap of paper and let out a low whistle. At the rate of replication now, as the virus gained momentum, the pack might die from the infection if it were given another week or so to proliferate further. Their only hope would be their offspring, for the virus oddly did not seem contagious. He doubted whether the pups, at so fragile an age, would be able to survive without the others. He wished it were not so; the wolves had escaped the lab only to bring it with them into the wild and die there. He wondered if that fate was so much better than if they had died on the operating table.

He called Haxler over and informed him of the news. The scientist cursed, not because of any fear for the wolves, but because without a full display of specimens he would not be able to show as much evidence and thus get as much money from the manufacturer. Haxler told Barnes to confirm his results, and to operate on the body, removing the implant to analyze what was left of it.

Haxler stormed into the back room and stood there, away from Barnes, deep in thought. So, the big black wolf would die eventually. But he would not get to kill him personally, and that was what Haxler wanted: to look the beast in the eye as he pulled the trigger, watch it fall limply to the ground. The rifle with which he had shot at that wolf was mounted on the wall, its wood finish cracked and splintered. Haxler recalled waking up after plunging into the dark abyss of unconsciousness to see the preparation table in shambles. Broken glass and fallen cages, some with dog subjects still in them, lay everywhere. He could see the bones jutting through his legs, could feel where the glass had cut his skin. The wolf was gone. He passed out, then awakened again, this time in the emergency room.

"You don't leave your enemies alive, wolf," muttered Haxler. "I don't know why you did it; maybe you knew I would suffer. You'll pay for your foolishness, though." He stroked the rifle lovingly, turning his hand over to look at the jagged scar which ran across it from a piece of glass. "You will all pay."

Rapid's memories were playing through his head as he emerged from alongside the old road in front of the lab. Exhausted into near delirium, the black wolf imagined that he felt Paloke's warm fur beside him and nuzzled closer. Then she was there in the meadow, her fur shimmering. Rapid stared curiously before either of them said anything. He could not comprehend the hallucination. "Mother, why have you come back? What is wrong?" He looked sorrowfully at the deadly fenced prison, which seemed to call to him, ushering him toward it. He stared down at his paws, noticing how good it felt to move them. He doubted he would have that freedom much longer. "Soon I will join you."

Her voice came back to him, more to his mind than his ears. "That's just it, my son. You aren't going to die. The *Aynsen* won't allow it. You will survive because of your inner courage. Yes, you will not die, but you will be hurt."

"But I will finish it, won't I, mother? I need—"

"You need not vengeance against Haxler, even if you think you do! You may attempt to disobey the will of the *Aynsen*, but no matter what happens, you will not be able to confront Haxler and gain closure. Man shall end himself. My son, you are strong in your soul, strong with the Earth. Use your strengths. It is up to you to save the pack now. Do not worry about retribution; it is not the place of wolves to seek it, though it shall be granted. Your quest is one of hope."

The image of his mother disappeared. Rapid did not know what to make of his hallucination, but continued toward the lab. He breathed deeply and stepped with purpose. If the *Aynsen* would protect him, so much the better. He would obey them, and not seek vengeance against Haxler. But he would not depart until he knew what was wrong with his pack.

His stomach was empty, but that was not why it churned. He mulled over the experiment. The sickness was a recent development, but the Copperleaf had noted something different with themselves immediately after the scars had appeared on their tails. Rapid knew that using intellect over instinct to the extent that they had been doing in the past few months was not the natural way of things. Timber was right: he never before would have connected so many different issues to arrive at the conclusion that he must go back to the lab and seek a remedy for their sickness.

Rapid put his paws up to the window and peered into the lab, seeing Barnes and Haxler within. Salyr was caged inside as well, and Rapid hoped fervently that his friend had not fallen victim to their experiments. Glen's Death scent was strong here, and as Rapid looked closer he could tell that Barnes was standing over his father's dead body.

The black wolf watched as Barnes started to perform an

operation. Rapid was stricken as he saw Glen's lifeless, ravaged body upon the table. His father, even in death, was not free of the men. Rapid bit back a howl of anguish and kept his mind upon the operation, watching how Barnes dug the implant out of the tail. As the man finished, Rapid's paws dropped from the windowsill and he turned to depart. He knew where in his tail the implant was, and his instinct told him that if he removed it, he would have a chance to live. He could return to the cave to tell the others, and they could all dig them out of their tails and be free of the lab's influence at last.

Then he thought of Salyr. He was doomed to die within a matter of days; the tests on dogs were much more harsh and often had lethal results. Yet actually entering the laboratory would be madness; the wolves had never been inside while conscious, and there was no way to get Salyr out of the cage at any rate. Rapid loped across the road, his head bowed, as he heard Salyr's bark; the dog had no doubt caught his scent. "Goodbye, old friend," he whispered. "I cannot save you."

Barnes finished working on the old male and was about to put his body back in the cooler when he heard a soft noise outside the lab. He looked out the window to see a wolf walking slowly away from it, as if he had been nosing around for some time. Barnes's heart caught in his throat. It couldn't be one of the wolves from the captive pack. It simply wasn't possible. After all that Haxler and he had subjected them to, and their last position up by Washbourne Lake, it didn't seem possible that one could be here now, no farther than ten yards from the window. Was this wolf searching for the old male? Jonathan squinted, trying to make out the shape now vanishing in the darkness. It seemed to be the smaller black male, the one he had seen by the bank hiding with the pups. Could it be that he was the last one left? Barnes had another attack of conscience; it seized him a thousand times a day: how cruel they were to the animals, how purposeless it all was, how they hunted down the wolves though they didn't pose any threat. . . .

He was startled by Haxler's cry of alarm from the back room. The scientist rushed out, loading the rifle, and darted out the front door. One of the dogs behind Barnes barked sharply. "Stop!" was all Jonathan could muster before he heard the report of the rifle and saw the wolf stumble in its tracks. It increased its pace, limping visibly, before dropping from another bullet. Jonathan raced out into the rain. It was over now, he knew. They had killed the last one. When they had caught the pack, there were eleven wolves, and he and Haxler were responsible, directly or indirectly, for the deaths of every one; even the pups, how many ever there were.

Jonathan tackled Haxler with barely controlled rage, striking him again and again, tearing the gun from his hands. Haxler's black eyes blazed beneath his graying locks, and he knocked Jonathan away, rising up in pain. "So, this is what it comes to? Your damned morals getting in the way again? What does it matter to you anyway—they've done you no great service, they don't count for anything! They're just a nuisance, a plague that needs to be driven out of this land!"

"You heartless. . . . You'll never understand," said Barnes, almost crying in the rain. They were both sprawled out in the mud, trying to get up, but their emotions, so intense, hindered their efforts. "They can think and feel! The dogs, back there—they can as well! And every day we carry out these godless tasks which would turn the stomach of every decent person on the earth, and for what? Science? Hardly. Most of these experiments aren't even worth a damn, but some little spark of consciousness dies for every one that we perform!"

"So what?" cried Haxler bitterly. "They'd have died in the shelters too. Or on the streets. Or on their master's hearth, when they've been nothing but a sinkhole for him to throw his money into until they're old and worthless. At least here their death serves a purpose!"

"Purpose? I question your definition of the word, when you just killed that wolf merely because you saw it! Even the wolf hunt arguably had a reason, though I hated it; we needed to cover our tracks. But this—this is merely your petty revenge, and I won't stand for it." Tears mixed with the rain on Jonathan's cheeks.

"It's not about revenge!" Haxler lied. "It's about these!" he said, motioning at his prosthetics. "It's about what *they* are capable of. I thought they were harmless enough at first, but you didn't see his eyes as he leapt at me: they were filled with fire and rage, and his teeth flashed silver as they went for my throat. Your naïveté is your failure, *not* mine, and so I must carry out the crusade alone! We must be rid of them, lest they bring the same fate upon others." Haxler saw Barnes's eyes and knew he was losing him. "Besides," he added slyly, "The more bodies we get, the more money we gain. Money that's hard to come by around here, even with your veterinary job."

Jonathan wished he could escape the siren call of the dollar, yet he knew its chains, though weakening, still held him down steadfastly. He cursed the money silently, cursed the fact that Haxler constantly was able to use it against him. Then he lifted himself out of the mud, walking over to the slumped wolf. He noticed it was still breathing and that its wounds were not fatal, letting out a sigh of profound relief. As Haxler realized this, he lifted the rifle yet again, aiming for the animal's head, but Jonathan reminded him that the wolves were worth more money if live studies were performed. Haxler had to make sure that it was not the wolf that had taken his legs before he lowered the gun reluctantly.

"Fine, we'll bring it back inside; do what you can to fix it up and then throw it in the pen. I don't have any more tasks for tonight, so lock up when you're done." Haxler was obviously upset at the altercation with his only co-worker, and quickly drove down the road. He muttered derisive comments on Barnes's righteous ways to himself on the drive home, for he knew that beneath the mask of ethics, Barnes was puppet to the dollar, and could never forsake its hold on him entirely.

Maya had awakened in the night and heard whispering. It sounded like two of the older wolves. She listened to the hushed whines and peeked out through one eye to watch their body language. She could not make out much; something about a journey, vengeance, and Haxler. She had not given it much thought and quickly drifted off again, but she stirred uneasily for a time before she arose to find Rapid gone, his trail old. He had been gone for quite a while.

Grabbing her precious elk bone, she followed her brother's trail intently. A rabbit, frightened by the storm and too frantic to get to the safety of its burrow, wandered into Maya's path. She stopped to feed upon it, for she decided that wherever Rapid's scent might lead her, she could use the strength.

Though Maya was stricken with illness like the other adults, she strayed from the trail frequently to investigate points of interest. This, along with her much slower trot, kept her from closing with Rapid until several hours after he was captured. Maya's stubbornness was her guiding light, for without it she would have succumbed to the spreading sickness long before reaching the lab. Though she did not feel her usual self, she dismissed the pain in her typical light-hearted manner, and carried herself as if she had an excess of energy nonetheless.

Rapid looked around him. He was back in the prison den, behind the electric fence. Blood oozed from both his wounds. Daybreak crept over the meadow subtly, not daring to truly push through the clouds. The *tanah* could not walk. His left hind leg and right haunch had been shot. He dragged himself along on his front two feet, hearing Haxler's car as it departed. The rain kept on pouring, and harsh winds bit through Rapid's soaked coat and open wounds. He moaned softly, putting his head on his paws, and watched the meadow as he used to. It was as if all that had happened since the pack's escape had never occurred.

Presently, small, quick pawsteps approached him. He looked up to see Maya, her face full of mischief, though her gait attested to her sickness. She gripped the elk bone firmly in her jaws, despite the long miles she had had to bear it. Her golden eyes were fixed on the lab, and Rapid could smell that she was fighting to control her fear with every step.

"Maya! What are you doing here? This is madness!" cried Rapid. He had taken her as his ward at her birth and was fearful for her safety. At any moment the other man could rush out and shoot her as they had him.

"Hush, you old fusspot," she panted. As was her wont, she made light of the situation by attempting to ignore it. "I'm not even going to ask what *you* are here for. Are you all right?"

"Not really," he said after wincing. "I've got two of their gun-stones in me, and I think I might have a broken rib. Have you been feeling at all sick lately? You must answer me honestly, little one. Now is no time for bandying playful words."

"A bit," Maya confessed evasively, like a child who is trying to avoid the truth by downplaying it. "It's like a lack of energy . . . nothing that won't pass soon."

"This isn't a pup-sickness, Maya," Rapid said sternly. "The humans are responsible. It won't go away unless we do something about it. I think I know what must be done, but I need you to show the others for me." Maya nodded gravely.

"There is a little scrap of metal in our tails that is making us ill. We've got to gnaw it out, but it's quite small and very deeply rooted, so you must observe its location carefully to tell Timber and Coast."

"Will it hurt, Rapid?"

"Yes. I'm already in a lot of pain, and I'm sure Haxler will be back, so I think I'm fairly done for. Salyr's been caught, too. But don't cry, little wolf. There is nothing that can be done to save us now. With you it is a different matter." Then Rapid began to dig the implant out with his teeth while Maya watched fretfully.

Rapid whined in agony as he spat out the CDL implant. "Do you remember where it was?" he asked, barely conscious. His ears were turned back and his eyes rolled randomly. His black body shook uncontrollably.

"I do." She gazed in pity with golden eyes at him.

"You must tell the others about it, and then you must all do this. It is an excruciating process, but it is necessary."

"Is the fence still bad?"

Rapid lifted his ears, rotating them slightly. "Yes, you can hear the bees humming."

"I'm going to leave you with a present," Maya said. Carefully she slid her coveted bone through the fence. It dropped on the other side. She stared at her brother through the chain links. "All that stuff about not coming back was just a joke, right?"

"No, I . . . Yes," he answered, smiling reassuringly. "It was, Maya. No need for alarm. See you tomorrow. Tell everyone I love them."

Maya risked slipping her muzzle through the fence to lick him. "You're the best brother I'll ever have."

"You're the best sister I shall ever have. Now get going before Barnes sees you."

"Goodbye," she said, falling back into the forest soundlessly.

Rapid lay where he was, lapsing in and out of consciousness, his tongue licking the bare bone. How could Paloke and the *Aynsen* expect him to survive this? His whole backside was in intense pain. He managed a half-hearted search of the bullet wounds. His hind leg was broken, but the bullet had passed clean through. His rear, however, had a bullet lodged inside it. His head dropped to the ground, staring at the bone as he whined piteously, and soon he fell to troubled dreams.

The slim black wolf lay unconscious in the pen, exhausted from its endeavors. Barnes opened the door and knelt down to look it over. He gasped at what he found, for even though he had earlier temporarily staunched the flow from the bullet wounds, the wolf was nevertheless lying in a pool of blood. He found that the wolf's tail had been torn apart and the CDL lay on the ground nearby. He carried the wolf inside quickly and lay it on a table, blinking back his own impending exhaustion. He acted with haste, extracting the bullet and binding the wounds as best he could, then looked with perplexity at the wolf. How had it known where the implant lay, if it had not watched Jonathan extract the CDL from Glen? The reasoning process required to make such a deduction startled Jonathan; he hadn't believed an animal capable of such a feat. His guilt at his actions in the lab only increased tenfold by this insight, and he petted the silky black coat mournfully.

Struck by this new revelation, Jon Barnes forced himself to think again upon all the horrific experiments he had carried out over the years in the name of science, and was stirred to shock as he imagined these complex, reasoning animals suffering by his hand—and fully conscious of his part in their deaths. All of this for money, and for the security that money offered. Suddenly something snapped inside him: whatever the consequences, he could never accept another paycheck in return for work that he now knew to be cruel and unnecessary. He would starve rather than continue working for Haxler. Jonathan felt after many years that he had finally gained a greater deal of control over his life than he had ever had before.

He realized that in the morning Haxler would return, and hearing that Rapid had removed the implant, would not marvel at the wolf's ingenuity, but only conclude that it had outlived its usefulness and must be shot immediately. Jonathan promised himself that he could not let that happen. Gently cradling the wounded black wolf in his arms, he carried it into the woods beyond the meadow and laid it down to rest amidst the trees. Its breaths seemed to become deeper as it inhaled the forest air, and Jonathan nodded contently. Then he returned to the lab, collected his things, and drove away, resolving never to return. Let Haxler carry out his canine experiments, if he could do so unassisted. On his head alone would rest the burden of future sins. Jonathan would do what he had intended all along: to simply be a vet, saving animals with medicine rather than killing them.

Chapter Thirteen

Sprint stretched. It was late afternoon in the second day the Copperleaf were at the cavern. The storm had finally abated. The little wolf nudged Coast, asking if she could play, then darted out of the cave. She lifted herself almost painfully from the stone floor of their new home and was struck by a slight bout of nausea. She felt colder than she used to after the long nights and wondered why.

Coast stepped out into knee-deep mud, for the ground had been thoroughly soaked. She had not seen Rapid or Maya and assumed they had gone hunting. She braced herself as Sprint leapt with a playful snarl, pushing her backward. She reeled into the cave, rolling over Timber. He awoke with a start. "Rapid?"

"No, it's me, Coast. You haven't seen Rapid or Maya, have you? Do you think they went hunting? This is the second day they're gone!"

Timber's body language became muddled in his confusion. He had slept through both days, though his rest was plagued with nightmares, as he was exhausted from scouting and the trek in the storm. "Maya? She . . . she . . . she's not supposed to. . . ."

"She's the age to hunt, or have you so soon forgotten?" she licked the bewildered wolf's muzzle and picked herself up. "Rapid, like the dutiful 'uncle' he is, probably took her out by the mountains. After she got hit by the elk the other day, he probably figured she needed to strengthen her hunting discipline."

"But . . . yes . . . he probably did."

"Do you want to join Sprint and me in a game of tag?" The concept of tag is almost universal in its appeal, and wolves play a form of it, trading nips and then darting away from each other.

"Er, no, I'll go look for them," Timber said, avoiding eye contact.

"Why?" asked Coast, realizing he was hiding something. She looked at him searchingly with her passive emerald eyes.

Maya loped in, panting heavily, and exclaimed, "Because Rapid's trapped in the lab, and Salyr with him!"

"What?" Coast barked in surprise. Timber whined miserably.

"It is true. The sickness we have all been silently bearing was troubling him, and he knew that it was caused by the humans. He left last night to find a cure. A futile quest, I know . . . I should have stopped him!" Timber growled. He began to cough uncontrollably.

Coast was at a loss, and sank to her belly in confusion. "But . . . how could he hope to figure out how our illness would be put right?"

Maya barked to get the others' attention. "He found a way. It's extremely painful; we have to wound ourselves. The humans put a small flat stone in our tail, and Rapid says that it is the source of our troubles. Each one of us has to gnaw it out."

"Were the pups spared, as they were yet unborn?" Coast asked weakly. Maya nodded. "That, at least, is some consolation," she sighed.

Timber stormed down the hill towards the town.

"I must find Rapid and Salyr and save them from the lab. I can defeat Haxler if needs be, as I have done before. Maybe I'll get shot down in the attempt, but it's fine by me. I've seen my days. I can't live without Rapid, and there's no one I'd rather die beside than him."

"You don't have to go alone," said a voice from beside him. "I'll think of this as my initiation," said Sprint, smiling.

"What folly has taken you?" demanded Coast. "You're barely two months old, and I'd be damned if you could cross a distance like that at the pace Timber would go! No, you'll stay here."

Timber saw something of the Old Wolf in Sprint then, some spark of Glen's courage, of his stubbornness. Timber knew that if he went alone, his rescue attempt would be suicidal, but he felt that the pup would somehow aid Timber with his presence. "Come on, then," Timber said, giving him a wolf-grin. "But you'd better keep up; I shan't want to stop just for a youngster like you. If I have to leave you in the Barren Lands, I will." The two disappeared between the firs before Coast knew what had taken place.

"Are the whole woods mad today?" she asked, baffled by what she had seen. Maya stumbled as she approached to comfort her sister, and Coast supported her, for the young wolf had traversed mile upon mile as she had traveled from the Cloud Tree to the cavern, then to the lab and back, in less than two days.

"I must show you how to remove the implant," Maya said.

"Rest now," replied Coast, reassuring her sister that there would be time enough after she slept.

Haxler took off his jacket. It was unnaturally quiet in the lab, though the dogs were whining in their kennels. He called to Barnes several times; then, receiving no answer, looked in the back room and realized that the young man wasn't there. He limped to the wolf pen, in order to check on the black wolf, but found only a small pool of blood in the dirt. Haxler looked closer and spotted a CDL, covered by dust. He cursed and turned to the meadow, hoping to see the wolf. Then it came to him: Barnes had removed the implant from the wolf and freed it, angered by last night's argument. Haxler threw the CDL over the fence, so that it fell among the meadow flowers, and stormed back into the lab. He saw a note, taped to the surgery table, in Barnes's handwriting.

'*I am sorry that I've had to leave you on your own in this. It is a difficult job to do without someone else there to help you rationalize its worth. I've come to the understanding that these animals are truly capable of interpreting the world around them just as well as we do, and the thought of performing these experiments on beings with such sentience does not sit well with me. Do not try to lure me back with the promise of more money: I value life above it. I had to take the wolf and return him to the forest where he'd have half a chance; I know you'd have shot him given the opportunity. You may do what you will with the dogs. Though I had to fight the urge to free them as well, I know this is your livelihood. I hope in time you will come to understand how fundamentally wrong this all is, and that you will harbor no ill will towards me for my decision. Ours are two very different viewpoints, and though I do not despise you for yours, I cannot go against mine any longer.'*

Haxler crumpled the paper, throwing it at one of the cages and sobbing in rage. How could Jonathan have done this? To leave him all alone? It wasn't right, Barnes taking on this tone: Jonathan's morals were no better than his own! He had worked at the lab for a year, and carried out tasks every bit as horrific as the ones Haxler himself had performed. '*Let him go, then,*' thought Haxler to himself. '*I'm the only one for this job.*'

Unable to stay in the empty lab any longer, Haxler stumbled through the door, neglecting to feed or give water to the dogs, or even to lock up, and drove off towards the nearest tavern.

Rapid, unconscious, began to dream. He was watching a river as it trailed down the mountainside, the wind blowing it in wisps like a veil. Howls sounded all around him, far more beautiful than he had ever heard before. As he was about to join in, a voice cautioned him, "You are yet alive, and cannot take part in our song." Then the *tanah* realized that the tundra below him was filled with lost wolves, untold masses of them. He could sense that they had all died at men's hands.

He awoke to see the sun's rays sinking below the pines. He blinked, trying to recall where he was. Rapid could not remember arriving in the woods, here along the Laibrook, nor what had happened beforehand. He had been given pain pills by Barnes, and they made his mouth feel dry and scratchy. He coughed, feeling the broken rib shoot pain through his side, and stayed in place for some time, staring at a lone flower inches in front of his face. Suddenly, the memories came upon him. He had left for the lab and seen how to remedy his sickness. Too late had he noticed Haxler rushing out of the lab after him, and the man had shot him—twice. He had fallen unconscious, the strain far too great, to find that Maya had joined him. Then he had operated on his tail himself, ripping out the implant to show Maya where it hid. She had left, and he had again slipped away from consciousness due to the pain. He had a brief memory of being held tight to Barnes's chest, trying to push away with his front paws, but other than that . . . nothing.

The realization that the human must have set him free caused Rapid immediate suspicion. What had they done to his body this time? He saw that his back leg was in a cast, and his tail and haunch wounds were dressed, but he did not realize that the bandages were meant to aid. He only saw them as another foul experiment, and tore them from his body with great pain, lying down again and gasping uncontrollably.

Rapid closed his eyes and focused his attention inwardly, listening to his body. The sickness was still there, but it had not worsened, and he felt that with time it would now fade away. He sensed no other real disturbances in his body, concluding that the cast and dressings had been the test for which they had set him free. He realized that the humans would know where he was as they had set him here. He began to drag himself along with his front paws, his jaws slack and tongue lolling, trying to get back to the cave. He had no doubt that it was an impossibly long journey; the Barren Lands would take at least three days to cross in this condition, not to mention the long miles beyond them.

⊠

"You hold up well, Sprint," praised Timber. "I truly doubted that you would be able to make such a journey. It is not even morning, and we have already crossed the Barren Lands."

"You don't seem fit for it yourself, Timber," Sprint said. His older brother's body looked as if he was dragging some massive log behind him. Timber had never before been fatigued, and Sprint worried about this. If Timber should suddenly weaken here, while they were so far into human territory, what should Sprint do? He was but a young pup, and would not know how to find his way back to the others.

"We are coming upon the Dark Place. I can smell the stink of *teyen* and chemicals upon the air. Rapid is near, as well," said Timber cautiously.

"Nearer than you think, *Honovi*," said a weary voice beside them. "Your senses are not what they once were. The sickness is growing in you."

"Rapid!" Timber said in amazement. "How have you escaped yet again? Maya said you had been captured." The big wolf noticed his brother was lying down, unmoving, in the brush. "You are wounded!"

"It was Haxler," panted Rapid in exhaustion. "He shot me twice. And I removed the implant, as you were supposed to. The men . . . performed another test on me . . . but I foiled it."

"You are truly meant to be the *tanah*," Timber said with reverence. "What of Salyr?"

"He is captured, within the lab with the other dogs. I do not foresee how we can get him out. Escape from the pen was difficult; escape from the lab itself is impossible."

"Yet I must try to save him. He is part of the Copperleaf."

Rapid affected a bemused smile. "A *teyen*, a Copperleaf? My, this is quite a change. What will the Earth come to, when such a thing happens? Will the mountains fall, or will bears spring from the lakes?"

"I see their tests could not do away with your sense of humor. It seems a pity, after all the other things they have done to me, that they couldn't have granted that one small favor," retorted Timber. "I cannot deny that Salyr is a Copperleaf, and he has shown his bravery many times over. I have seen many wolves incapable of the feats he has accomplished. That is why I must try to free him, even if I die in the attempt."

Rapid nodded and Timber disappeared behind him. "Sprint, I need you to accompany me. You must act as my guide back through the Barren Lands." Sprint whined that he would not be able to go to the lab, but his attention was soon riveted on the important task of acting as scout for Rapid, prancing ahead to stand on his hind legs, knobby paws poised on a stump, as he looked for signs of danger. Rapid laughed at the little wolf's energy and dragged himself along a few feet at a time, alternately slumping in his tracks and pushing forward with determination as his only source of strength.

Timber shuddered as he approached the lab. He had forgotten how strong a feeling of dread surrounded his memories of the place, and the din of the dogs and the familiar artificial scents did nothing to calm his quickened heart. Darkness had fallen and automatic lights which lit the wolf pen in a sickly pall had activated.

He noticed that the front door was ajar and took an exploratory sniff. Barnes and Haxler were long gone. The human scents reeked of intense emotions, of anger and tension, and they made Timber wary. These were similar to the scent that Haxler had given off when he had shot Wrath in the tail during their escape.

"Salyr? Are you in here?" Timber whined, sticking his head through the door. He cast his eyes around the cages.

"Timber! Good of you to show up!" Salyr exclaimed heartily, his wounded lop-ear bobbing above his head.

"How do we get you out of this thing?" The big wolf asked, gnawing the bars experimentally.

"No, don't do that, you silly sod," said Salyr hastily. "You'll break your teeth on it. There's a much easier way; I've watched Barnes and Haxler do it enough."

"How?" Timber asked intently, looking back at the open door nervously. He felt that Haxler could come storming through at any moment, blazing with anger, to slay them both. "I don't want to stay here any longer than necessary."

"I know what you mean," whined Salyr, shaking slightly. "They haven't done anything with me yet, but I've seen the others. I can't imagine the horrors you fellows have been through. Now, there's a latch just above the metal bars. Your paws should be big enough to push it down; it will open the door."

Timber stared blankly, frustrated because he could not comprehend what the dog meant. "Latch? I don't understand your *teyen* words."

"Don't get your fur in a ruff! It's merely that little block on the top of the cage. Place your paw on it and push down." Timber did as he was told and Salyr was free in a moment.

"Quick, we've got to escape before Haxler returns," Timber growled, turning to go. The dog hesitated, looking at the other kennels. The other dogs looked out mutely, staring with amazement that someone had managed to escape their cage.

"Stay and help me get them out, will you?" Salyr whined, beginning to paw the latches of other cages and help their occupants out onto the tile.

Timber growled angrily, then went down the line, pawing open the latches with such haste that within moments all the dogs were free to go. "Well, they're out. Let them do with their freedom what they wish. Let's go."

Salyr paused, looking over the ragged band of mutts and purebreds. Many were quite disfigured or injured from the experiments done to them, and Salyr was sure that none knew anything about living in the wild. Suddenly he turned to Timber. "I understand why I was brought here."

"Wonderful. Tell it to us at the cavern," Timber said, pacing in the grass outside the lab.

"Perhaps I will, but I'll be a bit late in coming. I've got to guide these fellows back to town. A lot of them have rightful masters, and they escaped their yards and wandered too far, or were simply snatched away from home by Haxler. I'm not sure if their owners will want them back now, but I'm sure at least some will and it's worth a try. What d'you say?"

Halfway through Salyr's speech, Timber had paused in his pacing, one foot poised in the air, and remained staring with frozen eyes at the back of the lab. He pushed his way past the dogs, pawing at the cooler.

"Timber, wait . . ." Salyr said half-heartedly.

"Glen's in here, Salyr," Timber said, pushing himself up against the cooler. "Rapid was wrong—they didn't kill him. They just trapped him for another one of their damned experiments. We can save him . . . We can—" The cooler finally gave way and crashed to the floor, spilling out ice and Glen's limp body, his majestic pelt bloodstained.

"He's gone, Timber," Salyr said softly. The dogs looked on curiously, for none of them had ever truly known a pack bond before. Timber howled, startling several of the dogs backward, then licked his father's cold face sadly.

"It's true, then," Timber whispered, leaning his head on the bloodied pelt. "Rapid was right . . . Haxler had killed you." Then, mournfully, Timber grabbed his father by the back of the neck and dragged the body out to the edge of the pond. "You go on, Salyr. You can trace Rapid's old scent back to the cave. Help the others out until Rapid and I return. I wish you luck on your journey." The spotted dog gave a canine bow, then led his band of misfits slowly down the road. There was a last rite that Timber had to perform for his father. The gloom of night that surrounded him was reflected in the darkness that enveloped his mind. The sickness was coursing through his body, he could feel it beating him down, and his father

. . . he finally knew that Glen had been killed by humankind. He dug a wide hole in the pond bank, and there laid his father's body.

The massive wolf released a deep sigh. He hadn't seen his father die, hadn't seen Glen's will to survive when, a bullet already through him, he had dragged himself forward, disappearing beneath a mist of hooves and dirt. He hadn't seen the chaos afterward as Rapid and Salyr hesitated in shock, risking their lives as well. He had not witnessed the final moments of his father's life, and this, he decided, was the least he could do.

"The men never understood," Timber said after a pause, "that we were living beings too. We try to live our lives free of them, but they just keep on coming nearer, cutting into our land and slaying our children. Coexisting with them here is a futile cause; only in a place where humans have learned to understand and appreciate the wolf can the two live together. I'm not sure if there is such a place in the world. They say that we should not bother them, yet they invade our land and expect us to move. It does not make sense. Perhaps I do not understand humans, but I am sure that humans do not understand us. I wonder if you can help them to, in some small way. Then, it seems, your death would have a purpose."

Timber covered up the burial place, his eyes riveted to his father's face until the last possible instant. Glen had been put to rest, and then there was only silence.

Chapter Fourteen

"Stay up on your feet, now," Salyr encouraged Cougher. The little dog stumbled off the road, so exhausted that he barely knew where his feet were taking him.

The Labrador turned to Salyr questioningly. "Most of us are quite thirsty. When will we get our water? We used to get it, you know, right at five o' clock, but I don't see our bowls anywhere here, and as you are no doubt very much aware I see everything. We should have brought them with us, I suppose. What are you going to do about it?"

Salyr turned to him. "If you're so parched, just take a drink out of a puddle. Earth knows there are enough about."

The Labrador jumped as if startled, noticing the puddles around him for the first time. "My word! So there are." He lapped hungrily, and several of the others followed suit.

"We're in town now," Salyr announced. "The houses are right there. We'll just march on through, and those of you that had homes should try to remember where they are."

"Mine's not far ahead," said Cougher, motioning at a little green house with white trimmings. Ivy traveled along the front porch, and a wreath of dried flowers hung on the door. The small dog found new energy as he spotted it, and dashed toward the door, scratching at it intently. Salyr smiled to himself, and they all drew closer to the house, waiting as they heard the subtle sounds of movement inside.

A young woman opened the door, then let out a cry of surprise, sweeping Cougher up into her arms. Then she saw the band of dogs behind him and called up several more people from inside. They examined the ragged survivors, looking them over and noting that they had been operated upon and that many were in quite bad shape. Salyr listened intently to the words, but their tone seemed nothing if not caring, and he was comforted by the way they patted the other dogs on the head. When the people attempted to pet him, he simply backed away nervously, still staying with the other dogs. Then the humans coaxed the band along, further into town, while the younger woman went back inside, Cougher in arms, to make some calls.

As the dogs continued on their march, the people from Cougher's house continually paused to knock on other doors, and more townsfolk arrived. Salyr noticed that gradually his little band was getting smaller, until there were no more than six or seven of them left. The large group of townspeople convened among themselves, looking at the remaining dogs, and decided that they must have been strays originally. They soon brought out some water and meat for them, which the animals devoured hungrily. The people began to discuss what to make of their lost dogs' condition. There was only one place that could be responsible for their appearance—the stitched foreheads, the bulging glass-eyes of starvation, the trembling paws. The Animal Research Center that they had believed only tested wolves had in fact been testing dogs, even stealing them to do so. They grew angry, and soon the group became a mob, making their way toward Haxler's house.

Salyr, unaware of what he had started, was satisfied that the dogs would be treated well, and slipped away from the town, heading for the bridge. He had done his duty, but it was not his place to live amongst people.

Haxler awoke through a milky haze of tattered dreams and liquor, rolling himself out to the side of his bed in whatever dim afternoon light the drawn curtains hadn't happened to catch. The clamor of his dreams had not yet subsided, and he scratched his tousled hair, attempting to free himself of yesterday's vicious hangover. He put on his legs (there was not a day when he was spared the bitter memories this task evoked) and stumbled into the bathroom, pouring tepid water over his face, though the noise he had heard in his dreams did not seem to dissipate. There was a loud knock at the door, and he walked up to answer it with a sour face.

He was greeted by over a dozen townspeople, all screaming for his blood. Some held signs, like "*You're Killing Your Best Friend*" and "*Wolves Are The Enemy, Not Our Dogs*", others held dogs treated in gauze or casts. Haxler realized with disbelief that the dogs were from the lab, that somehow they had escaped, and that the townspeople knew from whence they had come. He wondered if he was still dreaming; perhaps this was all part of a particularly ugly nightmare.

"What do you want?" Haxler said amidst the shouts. "An apology?"

"More than that, we want to know *why*!" cried out one angry woman, holding a small white terrier that seemed to stare at Haxler accusingly. "You've stolen our dogs from our very homes, and for what? We thought you were supposed to conduct tests on wolves, *not* on our dogs!"

"You wanted the wolves gone at any cost," he retorted. "You would shoot them, strangle them, and poison them. You paid us to find the most efficient ways to eradicate them! But it's too dangerous and expensive to keep catching wolves. We've got to do *some* tests on dogs."

"Wolves aren't dogs!" a man in the mob persisted.

"What right do you have to kidnap our pets? Wolves are nature's killers, dogs are man's best friend," went up another cry.

Haxler waited angrily for the ensuing shouts to die down, his arms folded across his chest. "You're just like Barnes was. All of you. You're on a little righteous crusade because it will make you feel as if you're doing something noble. Well, wake up! Wolves and dogs interbreed—you're all living with tamed wolves in your homes! You've brought this testing, and far worse, upon the wolf pack you helped capture, and you killed seventeen of the animals yourselves several days ago. That was all right with you, because it was the wolves that suffered, not your own precious puppies. But guess what? You're all responsible for the deaths of canines! There's no real difference whether they kill their own meat or have it served to them on a plate in a home like little kings! I was there on the hunt. We shot the pups as they bawled for their mothers, closed the dens off as parents and cubs were burned to death within their own homes. Some of you were on that hunt with me. You know what we did. I don't feel a bit sorry for it, and I doubt you do either. Nor do I feel sorry for experimenting on your dogs. I know where I stand. The problem is, you don't—you're still living in some fantasy world where the two aren't the least bit related, and you can separate the issues in your minds. I pity you."

He turned to go as a rock struck the back of his head. He looked angrily at the mob, but they were dispersing, leaving him only with glares from dagger eyes. One man, no doubt the one who had thrown the rock, regarded Haxler grimly before departing. "No one appreciates the way you're trying to twist things. You're not welcome here any more. I suggest you leave soon, before people exchange the signs for something more effective at making a point."

Haxler slammed the door on the man, storming back into his house. Everything was falling apart. The world had turned against him, and for what? A few mutts and wild animals? As the room began to spin, it seemed as if the air was filled with howls and barks and the shouting of angry people. He could imagine the mob tearing him apart as he fell beneath their rage, the odd little dogs that should have stayed in their cages watching with mute curiosity as he died. In his delirium Haxler tripped, and the floor seemed to leap up at him like the enormous black wolf had, and he screamed for fear of the vivid memory. Tears streamed from his face, and he beat back the thousand voices in his head, human and canine, as he tried to rationalize his actions. He fell to simple repetitions to try and maintain a sense of stability, and he stumbled about his house whispering that everyone else was a fool, and that his experiments truly helped the human race, that they were all vital to existence and the only reason any of that mob was alive was because of his tests.

The tests had disintegrated into nothingness. First the wolves had escaped, then the black one with the CDL had been 'saved' by Jonathan, then the dogs had somehow been freed, and arrived in town in their current state . . . The more Haxler thought about it the angrier he became, and the more his mind convinced him that the one responsible for all the animals' escapes was Jonathan. It was Barnes's purpose from the beginning to destroy his life's work, that Haxler now realized. The vet's righteousness had only been an excuse for his actions, but behind them there was nothing but malice. There was only one thing to do now, Haxler supposed. His work and reputation were destroyed. He had nothing more in this world to lose. He grabbed the old rifle from its chest in his closet and walked quickly out the door, his movement filled with fell purpose and his face grim and icy.

Rapid opened his eyes experimentally, as if to make sure he was not in the lab. He saw all around him a vast clearing, where nothing but old stumps remained. He was in the Barren Lands, yet even realizing this did not unsettle him, such was his relief at being free of the Research Center. He lay quietly, drinking in the momentary calm, wondering how long it would last before his mind became filled with the worries and conflicts of the day. Granted, the struggle for food and the long journey ahead on two paws to the cave was a welcome change from the madness of the last few days, but they would present their own challenges nonetheless.

He began to feel anxious for Timber. His calm had been broken again by apprehension for the safety of a pack member. Rapid thought about the rest of the pack. He hoped Maya had performed the surgery in front of Coast, and that both had rid themselves of the human device. He also hoped that Timber had freed Salyr and was now lying a few inches away from Rapid and Sprint, curled beside them for a nap. Yet he could not smell his brother's presence.

The *tanah* eyed the stitches Barnes had sewn his wounds with. He was lucky, though he did not realize it; the others would have open wounds and have to take care to stave off infection. He prayed to the *Aynsen* that none would turn septic. When Rapid actually performed the operation, delicate though it was, he did not have to eat away much, a small hole perhaps one and a quarter inch deep had sufficed. From there, he was able to brush out the device with his tongue. It was a painful process, but a small price to pay to be rid of human meddling that was slowly killing his body. He could feel the healing process beginning already.

Rapid lifted his head, a dry leaf falling from his ear, and peered about the vast expanse. His nose twitched curiously, sniffing the air to find Timber's scent. It was nearing, and Rapid breathed easier, relaxing against the ground. He looked at Sprint, playing not far off. A small mouse bounded away from the young wolf, and then there was an abbreviated squeak before the pup settled down for a meager breakfast.

"Rapid!" a voice barked across the way. Timber was loping up to his brother, panting heavily. His head throbbed and his tail brought the pain of the *Nesnya*, but he was a strong wolf and it was impossible to keep him down. "Salyr is free, but . . . our father . . . I saw his body in the lab. It is done. I have laid him to rest."

Rapid licked his oldest friend comfortingly. "You are very ill now. Perhaps you should remove the implant."

"We must get to the cave before I attempt such a thing, whether it takes one day or nine," Timber said stubbornly. "I sense you are rested, so we should push on. It is foolish to try and cross this human-country while there is yet daylight, but we have no choice. We must get out of this forest graveyard by tonight. The three of us will be safer once we get to wooded land. There is yet a long journey ahead."

The mob had visited Jonathan Barnes's house as well, yet he had fared far better than Haxler had. Jonathan had asked simply for forgiveness, and had told the mob that he was no longer a part of the lab—he knew the great wrongs that were committed there, wrongs that his tormented soul could never wholly atone for. The people accepted his confession with a bit of disappointment, but he promised them that he would leave at once: these mountains were no place for him any longer. They were filled with the ghosts of his crimes.

As Barnes was packing upstairs, Haxler approached the house, rifle in hand, and entered through the unlocked back door. He looked about slowly with sunken eyes, but he saw nothing of the vet, and instead remained motionless to listen. He heard the rustling of duffel bags as they were packed full and made his way carefully up the staircase.

Then a strange thing happened.

Haxler perceived a black shape out of the corner of his eye as he approached the top of the first flight, and turned toward it. It seemed to him that, inexplicably, the black wolf that was so central to his hatred was standing at the bottom of the staircase, watching him calmly with glistening gold eyes. Yet its image was hazy, seeming to shimmer in a fogged mist, and it did not move. "Ah, so it is you!" Haxler whispered. "Look what you have done!" he said harshly, sweeping his hands over his prosthetics. "You showed me just how easily a pawn may dethrone his king, or a slave his master . . . Why couldn't you have died like the others? Cowered in the corner like you were supposed to? You struck me down . . . and then you lived on, every night, in my dreams . . . you had the audacity to live in spite of what you had done!" Haxler gritted his teeth so hard that he could feel his jaw buckling, and beads of sweat ran down his face. The wolf remained there, unmoving, its eyes never parting from his own. "You will die now," Haxler said grimly, raising the gun to his shoulder. "The dreams will end, and I will be free of this madness." As he aimed, Haxler's foot slipped from the landing, and he tumbled down the flight of stairs to the hard wooden foyer.

Jonathan Barnes heard the shot and rushed out. He found Haxler, a halo of blood around his head, dead by the entrance. His rifle lay beside him, and a bullet hole went through the bottom of the front door.

All was Silence.

It was late in the evening of the sixth day since Rapid had departed from the cave. Salyr found the pack in bad condition. Three pairs of eyes stared out at him from the darkness of the cave. A soft, wavering voice he knew to be Coast's spoke. "It is good to see you again, Salyr. But . . . you could not have chosen a worse time to arrive."

Salyr took a small step into the cave. "What has happened?"

"Rapid, Sprint, and Timber are all missing. They have gone to the lab, and I am sure that nothing good has happened to them. Have you brought news of them? How did you escape?"

"I have outpaced them, then," Salyr said to himself. "Timber freed me, and Rapid freed himself. Last I saw, they were all doing fairly well. I'm sure Maya told you of Rapid's wounds, but it looks as if he will survive them. No doubt they are returning as quickly as they can."

"Through the Barren Lands, I am sure . . . There is no other way . . ." said Coast sadly. "Yet we have more pressing concerns." She raised her tail to show him the ragged gash in it where she had gnawed out the implant.

"You could bring sickness upon yourself with a wound like that!" Salyr exclaimed worriedly.

"According to Rapid, we are freeing ourselves of sickness by cutting out the thing that lay there," Coast replied, pushing the small CDL towards Salyr with her nose. He examined it closely and curiously, for the moonlight struck it with a fascinating glint. He growled at it, then took it in his mouth and buried it outside. "Maya and I have both done this," Coast said. "So that we cannot hunt. I am sure neither Rapid nor Timber will be in any shape to hunt if they return. Maya and I are all right without food for a time, but it's a problem for Crystal."

"I can hunt for you," said Salyr. "Big enough game to sustain the four of us."

Coast said nothing, but Salyr could tell from her body posture in the dim light that she was not convinced. "I do not doubt your capabilities when hunting in a pack," she said. "But how do you expect to bring a deer or elk down without aid? We are in high summer now, and the fawns are no longer an easy kill, for they are fleet of hoof, and their mothers still remain to guard them."

"You shall see," Salyr said. "Sleep now. I shall watch over you."

And so the three wolves slept, and Salyr kept his vigil at the mouth of the cave, deep in thought for the welfare of his friends.

⊠

Salyr lifted his body into the morning's shine. He walked along in the forest, enjoying the fresh smell of the flora. Even after only his brief time in confinement at the lab, he was viewing nature with new eyes. He wondered how the wolves could have survived so long within those walls, and how nature must feel to them now.

After an hour of roaming, he picked up the scent of three deer. His nose told him that there were two females and a young fawn.

He broke into a panting run through the bushes, taking a shortcut across a small thicket. Within ten minutes he was looking at them as they grazed peacefully in the meadow. He could feel his blood running quick through his veins with anticipation of the hunt, as if his last had been a lifetime ago. Heedlessly, he leapt into the meadow straight for the fawn.

The chase continued until the sun was high overhead. Salyr ran down the fawn as the other deer watched in fear, creeping away to feed. They would grieve for the lost young, but next year life would have another chance. He dropped down in exhaustion, panting from the exhilaration of the chase. He was happy, and for a moment he forgot all about Coast's desperation, Crystal's hungry eyes, and the Copperleaf in general. He closed his eyes and savored the moment.

Reality came back to him. How was he going to tow the whole carcass back? He couldn't regurgitate his food like the wolves. Or could he? He could feel the primal blood running through his veins and ate his fill. He cleaned his paws and shredded the hide. Already, scavenger birds had appeared around him, screaming for their share. He grabbed a big chunk of meat from the side of the carcass and buried it near the lake. His hope was to cache what was left, so that he might save it from scavengers. By the time he returned to the carcass, half a dozen birds were feeding on it. He scared them away, and again they cawed dreadfully, full of indignant hunger.

Salyr tore another piece of meat off. The time it took him to go from the first cache to the carcass would never do. He dug again, now a bit closer, and to save time he left the ground open so he could store more meat in it.

When he reached the cache with the third slice of meat, he was just in time to see a small fisher run to its hole by the bank, dragging the second piece with it. Salyr chased it only to have his third piece stolen by a bird after he laid it near an aspen. Salyr turned away, head bowed. He was still inexperienced at this sort of thing, compared to the wolves. One cache and a stomach gorged with meat would have to suffice.

❖

"Take this," Salyr said as he laid down a solid leg of meat before Coast. Her tired eyes deepened with gratitude. She looked down at the gift.

"I cannot accept it. Crystal is starving."

"Share it with Maya," Salyr said, as if he had not heard. "I will look for food again later in the afternoon, when it is cooler. Besides, I have a meat cache a few miles from the den. I need not hunt afresh," he sat down to stare into Coast's eyes.

"What of Crystal?"

The pup was awake, staring intently at the leg of meat and the blood caked on the dog's muzzle. "Crystal, lick my muzzle," Salyr motioned, assuming the stance of a wolf newly returned from the hunt. Crystal rushed towards him, licking intently. The dog called upon long-forgotten instincts, summoning some past memory of what he was supposed to do. He retched horribly, churning his stomach muscles. They started to heave, and an unpleasant, nauseous feeling overcame him. Then, up through his esophagus came the meat. It was good, and the pup dived eagerly into it.

The old life flowed back into Coast. "You can do it! You can hunt for the pack!" she showered him with kisses, which he returned.

⁂

Dusk arrived. Coast whined softly at the entrance of the cave. "The eighth night approaches, and they still have not returned. I fear the worst."

Salyr watched the changing light as it played across her face. "As do I. They seemed all right when I left them, but . . . The Barren Lands are rife with danger for three wolves, especially with the town's current mood."

Coast whined sadly. "Let us not speak of such things. Watch over Crystal and Maya. I'm going down to the lake to have a drink."

"May I join you? I'm quite parched," someone howled further down the hill. It was Timber, walking resolutely to the cave. He still hadn't removed the implant. His gait was crooked and vomit was caked around his mouth. Behind him hopped Sprint, and further down the slope Rapid was crawling determinedly upon two paws.

The Copperleaf were reunited at last, and a commotion of joyous questions were exchanged between the seven pack members. There was a flurry of licking and sniffing, play-tumbling and jumping, snarls and whines. Crystal leapt from the den to tackle her littermate. Soon the whole pack was laughing, with not a care in the world. No more implants, no more lost kin, no more laboratory. They were together.

Sprint walked away from the rest of them into a flowery clearing. The wind blew softly, speaking silently to the wolves, telling them that no more storms would come for a long time. The trees positively glowed in the dusk light, and purple shadows nipped at the wolves' heels. The older wolves hushed, watching Sprint, his ice-blue eyes intent with purpose, finding his way up a large rock. Facing the falling sun, he pulled up his head, illuminated by a shaft of gold light. His mouth opened slightly, releasing a piercing howl. It was no longer the yowling of a puppy, but the call of a matured wolf. The long journey across the Barren Lands had changed him.

Maya soon followed Sprint, finding a log to climb upon, and joined him in the howl. The others gradually came into the clearing and joined in the song, and soon the air was alive with the call of the wolves. The people of Dolsty turned toward the sound with mixed feelings, both of fear and guilt, as it echoed through the mountains.

Salyr was caught up in the intensity of the howl. He breathed it in and his eyes glittered and danced with the music. He was witnessing the primal song, and it filled him with magic. He turned to Rapid, asking permission to howl, and the *tanah* nodded his head hearteningly. Salyr stood beside Maya and joined in, feeling as if he remembered far back in time to the beginning, when the notes to the song were written by the Earth itself.

Nearly a month had passed since the Copperleaf had reunited. Salyr was happy that he only had to hunt for the pack for a week. Timber, Maya, and Coast all recovered very quickly from removing the implants, for without the infection constantly being compounded, their bodies had a chance to fight the sickness. Rapid had started to limp about, but the speed which had given him his name was not to return.

The pack lay spread out in a patch of soft grass outside the cavern. The sky was a pale blue, portending the rising sun. "We agree that we are still too close to humans?" Rapid asked.

"They've proven that any place men and wolves live together, we die. We must head north and west, and find a home where we are free of humans forever," Timber said. The others whined in agreement.

"We never will truly be free, I don't think," Rapid pondered. "They'll come sooner or later, and then we'll have to move again. Whether it will be in our lifetimes or our children's, I am uncertain. When shall we leave?"

"Today is as good a day as any," suggested Coast. "We just hunted two nights ago. Let us simply slake our thirst, and we can depart." Rapid agreed and the Copperleaf dispersed. Rapid and Salyr went down to the lake together to get a drink.

"How do you feel about the journey, old friend?" Rapid asked with concern. "You are no *teyen*, but if you come with us, you may never again see another human. I have seen the yearning in you, and though you fight it, I know that some part of you wishes you could share the pack-bond with a person."

Salyr waded into the lake, letting the cold waters clear his troubled mind. "I have made important decisions in my life, but none so important as this. There is no going back. I will never return to the land in which I was raised."

"Salyr, it is now for you to decide your own path. Your help has been invaluable and you would be more than welcome to travel with us. You are a Copperleaf now. But the times come and go, and you must sort out your own loyalties, whether they be to land or to pack. We shall be leaving soon and once we depart, we will travel fast and far. You may stay here if you wish, but for us to remain is too perilous. You will not be forgotten if you stay behind. I thank you for my life, and those of the pack, for we would surely have starved to death this last month if not for you."

The spotted dog felt a great rift form within him. Gradually he pulled himself out of the Washbourne. "I have lived long amidst these mountains. Yet there are others, for it is a large world that lies beyond them. This valley is not my home; the Copperleaf is. Wherever you go, I shall follow."

"You are a marvel of your kind, Salyr. The *Aynsen* have favored you, for you are a dog gifted with the heart of a wolf."

The two packmates walked slowly back up the bank to summon the others, filled with their memories of the valley. Rapid looked proudly over his brothers and sisters; they had traveled long and hard through many perils to stand here before him, and doubtless they would have to pass through many more. Yet Rapid would be there to lead them, and they to support him. As the Copperleaf looked back from the mountains at the glint of the morning sun, they realized that for the first time, they felt confident of their future.

Wolf-Speak Glossary

aynsen – the spirit guardians of Nature

Hluri – Wrath's pack name, meaning 'wanderer' or 'lone one'

Honovi – Timber's pack name, meaning 'strong' or 'noble'

juipah – 'quiet one'

maisa – title for the alpha, or dominant, female in a wolf pack

nesnya – the forces which work against Nature's will, found in the pollution and waste the wolves do not understand

tanah – title for the alpha, or dominant, male in a wolf pack

teyen – domesticated, or held by man; usually a derogatory term for dogs or livestock.

NIK SAWE is a young writer who has studied the nature of the wolf for many years, and is a strong proponent of animal rights. He lives in Los Altos, California and is currently working on a second book. He may be contacted by e-mail through the publisher at dunhillpublishing@pacbell.net.

Order Form

Please send me:
___ copies of *Wolf Trails* @ $8.95 each

Add $2.00 shipping and handling for the first book and $1.00 for each additional book. California residents add 7.5% sales tax. Make checks payable to Dunhill Publishing.

Name ____
Address ______________________________________
City ________________ State ______ Zip __________
Country ______________________________________

Send orders to:
Dunhill Publishing
18340 Sonoma Highway
Sonoma, California 95476